*Hot Alphas. Smart Women. Sexy Stories.*

NEW YORK TIMES BESTSELLING AUTHOR

# LAURELIN PAIGE

paige press

Paige Press, LLC
Leander, Texas

ISBN: 978-1-953520-31-9

Editing: Erica Russikoff at Erica Edits

Proofing: Michele Ficht, Kimberly Ruiz

Cover: Laurelin Paige

# ONE

## JOLIE

*Past*

I DROPPED my highlighter at the slam of a car door, perking my ears for more tell-tale sounds of my father's arrival. I'd barely been able to concentrate on my Advanced Biology textbook, and the dread of being unprepared began to turn solid like a rock in the pit of my stomach. Daddy would quiz me on the reading, and with him, the only acceptable option was to have the right answers.

There was no exception for special occasions like today. He hadn't even acted like there was anything out of the ordinary about his trip to Bradley International. As if he went to pick up a new member of the household every day.

My window faced the backyard, so I couldn't see the car, and even if I could, the smart thing would be to stay at my desk and focus on my homework until I had it memorized instead of peeking out. Years of living alone with a cruel man had taught me well to make wise choices; had taught me the consequences of choosing otherwise.

It had also inspired a rebellious streak that dared walk an often dangerous line.

I eased my chair out from my desk, quietly so the legs wouldn't screech across the wood floor, and tiptoed to my bedroom door. He hadn't locked it before he'd left for the airport. Before Carla, he would have. It was one of the first things that had changed when my stepmother had moved in four months ago, a sign that he might be different with someone else in the house.

That hope had been short-lived. Things had gotten easier, at least. His attention wasn't always on me. He noticed less the rare times that I fell out of line.

What would he be like now that our household of three was going to be four?

As I eased the door open, I told myself that was the main reason behind my intrigue—it was about self-preservation. Nothing more.

But the truth was, I was deeply curious about Carla's surprise son. I'd only found out about him after she'd officially taken the title of wife. I wasn't clear when my father had learned about him—before or after they'd gotten married—but it had definitely been he who'd insisted on bringing him to live with us now, two weeks into the new school year. So he could win points with his new bride, I imagined. Or so he could show off how transformative his methods of education could be. Or so he could have himself a whipping boy.

It certainly wasn't out of the kindness of his heart. He didn't seem to have one.

Outside my room, I crossed to the balcony and stooped down to peer between the rails. Even on my knees, I could only see the bottom of Carla's body as she stood at the front door, her back pressed to it to hold it open.

"Why didn't you park in the garage?" she called out. She had to know by now that my father rarely parked in the garage unless it was winter, but that didn't stop her from the occasional nag.

Not for the first time, I wondered how long my father would let that go on before he put a stop to it. For now it seemed they were still in the honeymoon period.

If he answered her, I couldn't hear it, and I was more interested in the boy who followed my father in, heaving a large duffel bag along with him.

"Hey," Carla said, stopping him before he'd walked in far enough for me to see more than from his waist down. She let the door go so she could cross to him. "Aren't you going to say hello to me?"

He dropped his duffel, and it landed on the floor with a plop. "Hello, Carla." His tone was bitter, his voice deeper than most of the guys at school with a subtle rasp. Warm, though. A much different timbre than my father's whose tone was clipped and hollow.

"That's not how you talk to your mother."

I tensed. My father rarely issued warnings.

The boy couldn't know that, though, and he smarted off again. "I didn't realize I still had a mother."

I could tell from Carla's shaky sigh that he'd hit her where he meant to, but before she had a chance to say anything, I heard a distinct thud that I recognized as the sound a hand made when struck against the back of someone's head.

"I won't say it again, Cade. In our home, you treat your elders with respect."

I shivered. That rule had been beaten into me, and it was now evident it would be beaten into this boy too. I'd been pretty sure that was why Daddy had told Carla he was going alone to pick up her son, so he could inform him of How Things Would Be in the Stark House on the way back.

Apparently, Cade hadn't quite gotten the message.

He would. Just not yet. "I apologize, sir," he said with dripping sarcasm. "It's been so long since I've had a real home, I guess I forgot my manners."

I saw my father's feet as he lurched for Cade, but this time Carla stepped in between them. "He's had a long trip, Langdon. He'll be better after he gets settled."

*Keep your mouth shut.*

I didn't know if I was thinking it for myself or for Cade. Despite being a flight away, I could feel him warring with himself not to say more, the same way I was fighting not to speak up in his defense.

*It would only make things worse*, I reminded myself.

I was positive that even Carla's interference would have consequences, if not now then later.

A tense beat passed before my father backed down. "You can get settled then. Upstairs. First room you come to. The door should be open. I expect a new attitude when you arrive down here for dinner, which will be at six thirty sharp."

It was my cue to go back to my room, but I still hadn't caught Cade's face, and I thought maybe as he bent to reach for his duffel, I might catch a glimpse...

But he was too fast, grabbing the bag in a hurried swoop and then bounding up the stairs two at a time. He was at the top by the time I'd managed to scramble to my feet, and the second our eyes caught, I froze in place.

Because first of all, Cade Warren was not a boy.

Not like the boys I knew anyway. He was on the thin side, but he was broad, and he had scruff along his chin that actually looked capable of being a full beard. His jaw was chiseled and his cheekbones defined, and with his height, he could easily have passed for a senior in college rather than in high school. No, he wasn't a boy at all. He was a man.

And second of all, the real reason his intense stare had me pinned to my place was because Cade Warren was hot.

Generally, looks weren't something I noticed. I flirted and messed around with plenty of the guys at school, but that was always about me more than it was about them. I'd never really been interested. I'd never encountered one who made my heart speed up or my tummy flip or made me forget how words worked, and maybe it was simply because of the circumstances—me, caught spying; him, a stranger moving into the room down the hall—but looking at Cade made all three of those things happen, and now I was frozen and stammering and on the verge of a panic attack.

Plus, I was still wearing my school uniform—Daddy hated wasteful changes of clothes—and my lips were dry, and my hair was falling out of the ponytail I'd put it in that morning, and though he was in worn jeans and had been traveling all day, he looked a thousand times better than I did, even on my best days.

But despite me being nothing to look at, he was looking. Looking very intensely. Staring into me, and for the briefest of seconds, I was sure he could see all of me. All the lonely parts. All the dark parts. All the secret parts.

I wasn't sure if that made me feel comforted or scared.

"You're Julianna," he said. Not a question. I'd always hated the formal sound of my name, but I didn't mind it when he said it.

"You're Cade." Daddy and Carla were no longer standing in the foyer below, but I spoke only loud enough to be heard down the hall. I hadn't lost sight of the fact that I was supposed to be doing homework, and even if my father was distracted by Cade, I knew shirking my responsibilities wouldn't go unnoticed.

After the words were out, I wished I'd been even quieter. Wished he hadn't been able to hear me at all. *You're Cade. Great response, Julianna.*

*Idiot.*

He didn't react to my lame attempt at communication, seemingly more concerned with getting his bearings. "That your room?" He pointed his chin toward the door behind me. I nodded. "This mine?" He gestured now to the room in front of him.

I nodded again.

Now he looked toward the bathroom. "That just for me?"

Another nod. "I have my own."

He eyed the distance between us, thirty feet of hallway that passed by the bathroom and a guest room and a linen closet. "Plenty of space. You'll have no reason to get in my way."

With three steps, he was in his room, the slam of his door reverberating in the air.

I winced. Partly because Daddy didn't like slamming doors.

Mostly because Cade's remark had stung.

I didn't know there were pains that could hurt anymore. I'd grown numb to the slap of a hand. My mind went somewhere else during my father's darker tortures. But this—this I felt.

Maybe I'd thought there could be a camaraderie between us, me and this stranger. He could have helped carry the burden of living in the Stark household.

He could have made me finally feel less alone.

Stupid me. What was he possibly going to change? He wasn't here to save me. He wasn't a hero. He was only my stepbrother.

# TWO

## CADE

IT TOOK me less than twenty minutes to unpack, and that included going through the new uniforms that had been left on the bed and tossing the bag in the trash. Once upon a time, I'd owned more than could fit in an oversized duffle, but that was all I'd brought when my mother had dropped me off at Stu Goodie's house a little more than a year ago. I would have packed more if I hadn't been told I was only staying through the weekend.

Sometimes I wondered about the items that I'd lost in my mother's abandonment. Most were clothes I'd grown out of anyway, but there'd been a few things I'd cared about. The Nintendo Gameboy. A stack of Tom Clancy books. The keychain rabbit's foot that I'd had since I was five.

Well, they hadn't been waiting for me in this bedroom, which meant they were gone for good. I knew that without even asking.

A renewed sense of anger spiked through me as I slammed a dresser drawer shut. Why had I even bothered unpacking? Like hell was I staying.

I stormed out of the room and down the stairs and was grateful to find my stepfather nowhere in sight. Carla was easy enough to find. There was still twenty minutes before dinner, and having pegged Langdon Stark as a traditionalist the minute I laid eyes on him, I was sure she couldn't be anywhere else but the kitchen.

I followed the scent of baked ham and found her bent with an electric hand mixer over a bowl of potato chunks. Her expression hardened when she saw me, but she only spared me a glance before turning her focus back on her meal.

"Tell me again why I couldn't stay in Kentucky?" I circled around the kitchen island so that I could face her but still have a barrier between us when we did.

A *physical* barrier. There were plenty of less tangible ones already.

"Because I'm here," she said without even a pretense of patience. "And because you're my son."

"So?"

Any response she gave would be a trap, and she knew it. "I don't have time for ridiculous conversations, Cade."

"The only thing that's ridiculous about it is you trying to suggest that parents should be with their children."

She set down the mixer with a thump. "I wanted to be with you. I've told you why I couldn't be."

"Actually, no. You haven't. But no need. I get that it was easier to catch your next man without a kid weighing you down."

"I was trying to build a better life for us. And I did. Look around you. We never had this type of security before. We never had the life that Langdon provides." She went back to her cooking, throwing the beaters in the sink then turning to stir the gravy on the stove.

I took a moment to sweep my eyes over the gourmet kitchen. It wasn't as fancy as the ones that were in the houses in the Parade of Homes shows she used to drag me to, but it was certainly way above anything we'd had in the past. Shit, we'd never even owned a dishwasher when we'd been on our own.

The reality, though, was that we were never on our own for very long. And the men that were with us in between never stayed.

Granted, none had ever put a ring on her finger like this one had.

I glanced at the diamond on her left hand and the plain gold band beneath it. "Do you get to keep that when he leaves you? I bet you could get some decent rent money with it."

"You're ungrateful and self-centered. Just like your father."

There he was—my mysterious father. Half of the time, she claimed that he'd been a one-night stand. The other half, she claimed she wasn't even sure who he was. And yet she knew enough about him to identify his hateful qualities whenever it was useful to her.

I'd grown immune to the mentions by the time I'd hit ten. "I'm the one who's self-centered? Okay. Sure. How about I offer a selfless act then and volunteer to get out of your hair altogether. Let you enjoy your new family unit without any extra baggage."

"Don't be so dramatic." She turned off the stove, setting the cooked carrots on a cool adjacent burner. "We want you here. I want you here. I always wanted you with me."

"You disappeared for a year! If you wanted me, why did you abandon me?" I hadn't minded her seeing my rage, but I could feel a more vulnerable emotion bubbling up in my chest, threatening to burst.

"I didn't abandon you. I left you with a good family—"

"They thought you were going for a job interview. We didn't hear from you for four months!" And then another nine passed after that before she'd informed the Goodies she'd gotten married and could finally take her son back. "How is that not abandonment?"

"I was doing what I thought was best," she snapped. She stared at me, her gaze heavy and loaded, and I met her back with equal venom.

"How could you do that, Mom? How?" I hated the way my voice cracked and how my vision suddenly felt blurred.

She opened her mouth, and for the briefest second, I thought she might actually give me something real.

But then a timer buzzed, and she jumped back to her duties, grabbing mitts before heading over to the oven.

"It's complicated," she said as she took out the baking dish with the ham.

That's all it ever was with her—fucking complicated.

---

THE ONLY REASON I showed up to dinner ten minutes later was because I was hungry, and as much as Carla sucked at mothering, she was actually a good cook.

It wasn't at all to please Langdon Stark.

Sure, he'd huffed and puffed the whole ride, telling me about rules and manners and what to expect living in "his" house, but I'd seen this act before. Even the smack against the head wasn't anything new. Carla hadn't married any of her boyfriends before this one, but they all liked to assume authority over her son right off the bat, as if that quality would make them more attractive to her. Truth was, she just needed to have someone pay the rent, and she'd spread her legs. She couldn't care less if they were "good" with me.

Needless of my motivations, I walked into the dining room at six twenty-nine. The table had been set, all the delicious food my mother had been preparing now displayed in matching dishes. Julianna was already there, pouring water into glasses. She didn't even look up as I sat down across from her.

I chuckled to myself as the grandfather clock in the living room struck half past, and Daddy Stark still wasn't seated, but before the clock's song had ended, there he was, walking toward the chair at the head of the table with such precision, it was as if he were part of an automation.

My mother scurried in on his heels, her face red as she put down a tray of dinner rolls. "I'm sorry, Langdon. I didn't time the bread right."

Her husband gave her a disapproving look, but I had a feeling it was less to do with her two-second tardiness and more about me. The fact that all eyes had moved to me, the only one sitting, validated that feeling.

"Is this how you've taught the boy?" His admonition came out thick and ominous.

I had to shoo away the urge to protect my mother. She'd made her bed. If I got lectured along with her, so be it.

Besides, I honestly had no idea what I'd done wrong.

"He's been away for some time. He'll catch on quickly." She didn't look as sure as her words. She gestured toward me with her head, but I couldn't decipher her meaning.

Had I sat down in the wrong seat?

My mother started to explain. "We don't sit until—"

Langdon cut her off. "In a proper household, the master is the last to arrive, and the first to sit. As this is your first night here—and as you've likely been in a home led by less attentive adults—I'll give you an allowance for tonight's ill behavior."

"Wow, super kind of you." Was this guy for real?

His daughter's eyes went wide. My mother shifted nervously.

"Stop fidgeting, Carla."

Immediately, she became motionless. Everyone stood real still, waiting. It took a beat before I realized what they were waiting for. "You mean you want me to stand now?"

"I didn't explain how the dinnertime seating worked so that I could hear my own voice."

But hadn't he just said he'd give me an allowance?

I stood up, slowly, trying to decide if my mother's ham was worth this much trouble. When I'd been standing and nothing happened, I definitely was sure that it wasn't. "What did I fuck up now?"

My mother inhaled sharply.

*Forget this.* I was just about to ditch the bullshit when my gaze caught on the girl across from me. *Julianna.* My mother had told me about her in the same conversation that she'd told me about her marriage. A breath after she'd told me I was moving back, as though having a stepsibling might be enticing.

She hadn't mentioned that Julianna was also a teenager. Or that she had plump, raspberry-colored lips. And that her long, toned legs made a simple school uniform skirt look obscene.

Just my luck that my stepsister was a complete hottie.

It was her piercing blue eyes that kept me sitting there, and not because they were beautiful, but because they felt deep. Like what I saw was only wading in the shallows, and there was a whole ocean underneath. Those eyes were an anchor. They held me in place, and suddenly it occurred to me that leaving might be weaker than staying, and maybe this was a good time to show a bit of strength.

"Cursing in this house will be punished," Langdon said. "That will be your only warning."

"Like, you'll wash my mouth out or...?" I trailed off when I noticed Julianna frown. I'd yet to see her smile, and I was curious what that looked like.

Though with this hardass for a father, I doubted she did that very often.

Smarting off more didn't seem to be the way to go about seeing it, so I kept my trap shut. Tense silence strung out between the four of us as we stood at our places, waiting. Waiting.

"Could someone give me a little guidance here?" It was evident I was supposed to do something, and I still didn't know what was expected of me. The ham wasn't going to be any good if it was cold.

"Typically, when one insults their elders, it is customary for him to offer an apology." Stark had waited a handful of seconds before answering, almost baiting the others to answer first. I suspected that would have pissed him off, them talking out of turn and everything. I was starting to understand that this prick was after more than respect. He enjoyed this power game. Enjoyed the taunting and inciting.

He probably enjoyed the punishments that followed as well.

My mother had dated someone like that years ago, when I'd still been in elementary school. My middle finger on my left hand was crooked from an incident

with that prick. I'd carried a ball of dread with me in my
stomach the entire time Carla had been with him. I'd
never slept better than the night we'd spent in a shelter
after he'd kicked us out.

I was older now, though. In four months, I'd be old
enough to go out on my own. In eight, I'd have a
diploma. Whatever this asshole wanted to dole out, I
could survive that long. I didn't need to bend to his
whims.

Julianna's eyes stayed steady on me.

I found myself speaking before I made the decision
to apologize. "I'm sorry for my ill manners." Remembering a rule he'd given me in the car, I added, "Sir."

Stark's lips turned up slightly at the corners, but I
sensed he was more pleased with my discomfort than my
apology. "Not so hard, was that? Even the best dogs need
training. You're a quick learner. I can tell."

He sat down.

I was smart enough to wait until the women started
to sit before I followed suit, which they didn't do until
Stark had given a nod.

Once seated, I reached for a roll, only to have a fork
come swiftly down into the bread, centimeters from my
finger. "Surely, you are not in the habit of eating before
grace?"

The Goodies had been the pray-before-meal type as
well. "We served ourselves beforehand at the last place,"
I said, which was a lie but not something he'd ever know,
and did I really deserve to have my hand nearly jabbed
for the "mistake"?

"How vulgar." He genuinely looked a little sick at the thought. "Who will volunteer?"

He was staring at me pointedly, a not-so-subtle hint.

Before I had time to decide if I was going to let him bully me into doing what he wanted, Julianna spoke. "I will."

Stark's eye twitched, but when he turned his gaze to his daughter, he beamed. "Of course you will, darling. Setting an excellent example. I wouldn't expect anything less."

She smiled, pleased to have him pleased.

A rule follower. My instinct to keep my distance from her had been right then. Likely, she was the type to tattle. Headmaster's pet and his daughter as well. Ten bucks said she had no friends. I certainly wasn't getting in line for the role.

She bowed her head and started reciting a memorized prayer. I turned to look at my mother, a woman who had never prayed once at the dinner table when I'd lived with her in the past, and found her eyes closed and her hands clasped, her mouth moving silently as Julianna spoke.

Great. Ma had found God. As if she didn't have enough dysfunctional relationships.

Rolling my eyes, I glanced at Stark. He hadn't bowed his head, and his stare was fixed on me, his expression cold and hard and menacing.

Quickly, I lowered my head, in time to hit the "Amen" and lift it again.

Serving began the instant the prayer was over, but

only to Stark. Julianna placed a slice of ham on his plate followed by a spoonful of carrots. My mother stood and circled the table to dish him some mashed potatoes and gravy. It seemed I was expected to give him a roll since they were in front of me.

So I did.

Earning me a relieved smile from my mother.

When she sat down again, she waited expectantly for her husband to taste his food. All of it. Julianna sat still as well, though she was watching me, her face unreadable.

"Very good, Carla," my new stepfather said. "The ham is perfection."

I could feel her shoulders relax.

Then he went on. "Good thing it is too. It makes up for the lack of glaze on the carrots. And three starches in one meal? You know better than that."

She lowered her eyes. "The asparagus had gone bad."

"Then you'll learn to plan better. Won't you?"

"Of course."

He took three more bites before he motioned to us. "Go ahead. Eat up. It's already getting cold."

She and Julianna began dishing up their own plates. I waited until they were done, just in case there was a women-go-first rule I didn't know about, then served myself. Though, to be honest, I'd begun to lose my appetite.

Picking at my food, it began to return. The ham really was perfection. And the carrots were amazing the way she'd made them—with rosemary and oil. They'd been my favorite before.

I felt a softening toward her when it occurred to me she might have made them for me.

But then, out of the blue, she announced, "I'll do better, Langdon. I will."

"I know you will, dear." While I took those words as a threat, my mother glowed. As though fueled by her husband's support, ignoring the fact that she'd only needed it because he'd cut her down in the first place.

I knew then that I'd lost her. Knew that any hint of the woman who had once cared for me was gone. Knew that even if she'd chosen the carrots over the asparagus for me, she wouldn't do it again. That every choice after this would always put him first.

Once more I scanned the table—the do-gooder across from me, the stepfather with a need for control, the mother who'd abandoned her son.

I'd been without her for a while now. For the first time, I realized I was truly on my own.

# THREE
## CADE

"LOOK who's got the hots for New Boy."

I followed Troy's gaze to a group of girls in gym clothes walking the track, which was really just a quarter-mile gravel path that circled the school's main grounds. They were looking at us and giggling, suggesting they were talking about us as well, but I had no idea why he'd assumed it was me that had their attention.

"Which one?" Birch asked, more interested than I was. I'd already stopped looking.

"Amelia."

Birch nodded, as though his acceptance meant something to me. I hadn't decided yet if it did. He was definitely the popular man on campus, and befriending him would have its benefits.

Being a loner had benefits too.

Birch kicked at my shoe to get my attention. "Amelia

would be a good starter girlfriend, Cade. I can hook you guys up, if you're into her."

*Starter girlfriend.* "Fuck you."

He laughed. "It's not a comment on your experience, asshole. There's a hierarchy. You can't get to the top-ranked girls without proving yourself with the lesser."

"He's not dicking with you," Troy said in a way that suggested it wasn't unlike Birch to bullshit.

I leaned back against the shed, turned off by both the idea of a ranking system with the girls and the notion that who you dated was just another way to show off status. It was true in my last school, too, but after only three weeks, I could tell it was worse here.

That was the whole environment at Stark Academy, though. All that mattered was power, power, power. Not only did the curriculum enforce the belief, but most of the students came from family backgrounds that exemplified it.

I was definitely the odd man out. In more ways than I could count.

Birch misinterpreted my silence as hesitation. "Come by my room tonight," he said. "I'll tell her you need a tutor, then I'll make myself scarce."

There was no doubt he could make it happen. Not only did Antoine Birch have the face and charm that girls went for, but he also had a pedigree that made him influential. His father was president of one of the nation's premier banks. His mother, a notable French actress who lived in London. His connections had the staff wrapped around his finger, and there wasn't a student on campus who didn't jump when he told them how high.

I actually could use some help with schoolwork, a fact I wouldn't admit to the guys. I'd gotten decent grades in the past; not from trying. Natural instincts weren't enough to survive at a prestigious school like the one my stepfather ran. I wasn't made for it. Not because I was afraid of hard work, an accusation I'd already heard from his lips a time or two, but because I wasn't made to be reined in.

But getting out of the Stark household, even under the guise of being tutored, wasn't a task I'd figured out how to manage yet. The few attempts I'd made had ended in menial punishments. No television privileges one night. No dessert, another. A backhanded slap across the face a couple evenings before.

I preferred to be seen as a tough guy, but I didn't know if I had the stomach for it. I was fully aware that I'd only scratched the surface of Stark's wrath. I was already toeing the line by ducking out of study hall to sit out here and shoot the shit. I wasn't sure I was ready to push my luck with more disobedience.

"I'm not really interested in a girlfriend," I said finally, hoping the true statement would get me out of having to prove myself a rebel.

Birch pulled out a pack of cigarettes from his shoulder bag and stuck one in his mouth, a Zippo poised to light it. "What *are* you interested in? Fags?"

I cringed at the remark, even though I was sure he'd said it to be clever rather than homophobic.

"Fag. You get it? Because they call smokes fags in Britain." Troy was the perfect lackey. He'd probably suck him off, if that's what Birch wanted, and Troy had made it perfectly clear he was not into boys.

I ignored the invitation to pour praise on the top dog and answered the question. "Keeping my head down and graduating."

Birch passed the pack and the light to Troy. "Ah, I get it. You got a girl back home. Promised to be faithful?"

"No, no. I mean, there was a girl I fucked around with, but it wasn't like that." Well, it wasn't like that for me. I'd been clear from the start with Heather that relationships weren't my thing, which hadn't prevented her from latching on.

The sex had been too good for me to dump her altogether, but honestly, if there was anything good that had come from being suddenly transported to Wallingford, it was that I no longer had to deal with her constant attempts to make us a couple.

"So you want a fuck buddy." Cigarette lit, Troy passed the pack and the light to me.

I paused before taking one out. Though the shed and the grounds behind it were an area that seemed ignored by the adults, we weren't exactly out of sight.

On the other hand, I'd really missed smoking.

Fuck it.

I put the Camel between my lips and lit it. Then I set the pack and the light on the ground at my side. "I wouldn't mind a fuck buddy. If you could find me a chick that wouldn't get attached."

Birch looked back to the running path where the girls gym class was still walking the loop. "For that, I'd suggest *her*, but you know."

I took a drag as I again followed his line of sight and this time landed on Julianna. Her long hair was pulled back in a ponytail, her expression intent as she jogged past slower students. Her legs were more muscular than I'd realized. Her ass, more toned. She really was beautiful.

When she turned her head and saw me watching her, I smiled unintentionally. She didn't return it before moving her focus back to the path in front of her.

"Oh, yeah, Jules gives awesome head," Troy agreed. "You should definitely hook up with her."

Birch lightly smacked Troy's shoulder with the back of his hand. "He can't hook up with her, you moron. She's his stepsister."

"Right, right. It's not blood related, though. They could still get it on, couldn't they?"

Birch shrugged. "Kind of weird, if you ask me."

"Too bad. She's for sure the girl you want for no-strings-attached fucking around."

"You're bullshitting me." I'd spent as little time with Julianna as possible over the last month, which hadn't been hard since she pretty much stayed in her room and did schoolwork all the time that she wasn't in school or at mealtime. I had no doubt that my initial impression of her had been accurate—model student, model daughter, model everything. The image of her down on her knees did not fit into that notion.

It bothered me to even think about it. Which seemed strange. Maybe I had more brotherly feelings about her than I realized.

Except that didn't seem right either.

"No bullshit." Birch put a hand up as if to swear. "She gets around. Practically a rite of passage to have her lips on your dick."

"Have you fucked her?" I sounded more pissed than I'd meant to. I didn't feel quite angry, though. I felt something else, something I couldn't quite identify.

"He wants to," Troy said when Birch didn't answer. "He hates it when he's the only one who hasn't had access to something."

Birch scowled. "Like you've fucked her."

Troy shrugged. "But everyone else has."

I took another drag of my cigarette, hoping it would relax my suddenly tight muscles.

"Everyone else *claims* to," Birch corrected. "I don't actually know that anyone has. She might be a virgin with loose lips and that's all."

I didn't exactly feel relieved, but the tension in my shoulders eased slightly. "Does her father know?"

"That she's a BJ queen?" Birch stamped the cherry of his smoke out on the shed, then flicked the butt into a nearby trash can. "Fuck no. He'd kill her."

No shit, he'd kill her. "I'm surprised she takes the risk. I took her as a straight-liner."

"She usually is. Maybe she's hoping to get caught."

"Why would she want to be caught?" Troy seemed less aware of basic psychology than his friend.

Birch stood up and wiped the ground from his slacks. "I don't know. Some people get off on the taboo shit."

I barely knew her, but from my limited experience in the Stark household, I had a feeling it was less about taboo and more about control. It was the one thing she could decide for herself, and that had to feel satisfying. I could understand that. I could understand *her*.

If it was true, that was. I still wasn't entirely sure they weren't dicking with me.

Troy moved into a crouch. "You seen her titties yet, Warren?"

"Yeah, Troy. She parades around the house naked. Didn't you know?" I fought the urge to punch the guy in the nuts. I had a perfect opening. Such a shame.

He grinned, putting out his cigarette on the ground. "A guy can dream." He stood up. "You coming to Economics?"

I took a final drag, considering. It was tempting to ditch the rest of the day, but what would I do instead? No car, no funds, and a boarding school campus made for very few opportunities for fun.

Before I could answer, though, someone else answered for me. "He is not. He's coming with me."

I looked up to see the last person I wanted to see while I still had a lit cigarette between my lips—Headmaster Stark.

# FOUR

## CADE

"HAND THEM OVER," Stark said, his palm waiting.

For a second, I thought he meant the cigarette in my hand, but then I realized he meant the pack and the Zippo. I handed both over, then stood, swaying when I got to my feet. I'd smoked an occasional light back at my last school. The Camel was stronger than I was used to and made me especially jittery.

The anxiety of being caught doing something wrong didn't help my blood pressure.

"Who do they belong to?" Stark asked, eyeing the three of us. He lingered on me, a spark in his eyes despite his cruel expression before turning his focus to Birch. "You've been caught with cigarettes before. This brand, if I remember correctly. Are these yours?"

Logic said they weren't mine. If I'd brought them from Kentucky, it wouldn't still be a full pack, and when would I have had a chance to have bought them here?

But I was the only one still holding a smoke and too new to claim they belonged to anyone else without gaining a reputation I'd rather not have. Then, when Birch didn't respond, it seemed a clear message that I was expected to take the blame.

Fuck.

"They're mine, sir," I said, doing my best to keep my chin up and proud. If I was going to take the fall, I was going to be a man about it.

I swore I heard a note of glee in Stark's tone when he spoke. "Well then, Cade. It seems you will be accompanying me to my office. The rest of you—" He quickly scanned the small crowd that had gathered along. "Get to your next class."

Birch and Troy weren't even going to get detention for skipping study hall? Didn't seem fair. I supposed there was a chance he'd let me off as well when we were alone, that this was a demonstration to the school that he wouldn't play favorites, but from what I'd seen of him the last couple of weeks, the man didn't think he had to prove anything to anyone.

And even if he did, I certainly wasn't a favorite.

Resigned, I dropped the butt and stamped it out with my foot. Then made a show of putting it in the trash, determined not to add littering to my list of sins before following after my stepfather as he made his way to the administration wing of the main building.

We walked in silence, but there was plenty being said by others. Class had released, and students flooded the grounds as they hustled to their next hour. No one was too busy to notice the headmaster with a student in tow—his stepson, no less—and intense stares turned into rapid whispering behind our backs.

It had the potential of being embarrassing, though I couldn't decide who would be more scandalized by my crime. When I realized it was probably him, that the inability to keep his own stepson in line had to be quite a blow to his authority, the walk of shame became a lot less shameful. Soon I found a smug grin creeping onto my lips, emboldened by the fact that he couldn't see my expression when he walked ahead of me.

And what was the worst that would happen? I already spent all my evenings working on homework. I didn't have any possessions that I could have taken away. If my mother was upset, that might even be a step up in our relationship. It wasn't like I could get kicked out of school.

As for my peers, if they thought I was a bad boy, it was no skin off my back. If anything, a little trouble might make me popular. It would definitely improve my ability to get hookups to drugs and booze, and Birch and Troy had to have my back after I proved I had theirs. So I'd have to sit through a lame-ass lecture from my stepfather as punishment. All in all, it seemed worth the price.

My confidence only faltered when I saw Julianna.

She was back in her school uniform, a calculus textbook in her arms, her forehead still shiny with sweat from gym class. She stared, as everyone had when we walked by, but there was something else in her face—a flash of panic that had me craning over my neck to look

again. Her eyes met mine then, and while I could understand how a goody-goody would see any act of discipline
as terrifying, there was something about the fear in her
gaze that rattled me.

My smile dropped, and by the time we got to Stark's
office, my confidence was gone as well.

"Take a seat," he said, not bothering to look at me as
he went directly to the cabinet behind his desk, pulled a
ring of keys from his belt, and unlocked the top drawer
before putting the keys, the lighter, and the pack of cigarettes on his desk and sitting down.

I hadn't yet been to my stepfather's office. My
mother and I had spent an afternoon with the secretary
down the hall, getting my transfer in order, but when
she'd slipped down the hall to say goodbye, she'd gone
alone.

I took it in quickly—it was dark and wood paneled.
Cabinets and bookshelves lined three of the walls,
making the room feel especially small and confined. Not
that it was a very large office in the first place. The oversized desk took up a third of the space. Beyond that there
were three chairs—one large and leather on his side, two
plain armless chairs on the other. The only window had
the blinds closed, and the overhead fluorescents were
turned off, so the only source of light came from the desk
lamp and a floor lamp in the corner.

I turned my neck to find the only wall space was
behind me and covered with framed graduation certifi-
cates and certifications and awards, and I was still
looking in that direction when he spoke again.

"I said to sit down."

His tone was sharper this time, warning me it wasn't a good idea to point out that he'd actually said *take a seat* and just go ahead and do it.

Once seated, with his stern face looking at me disapprovingly across his desk, I felt smaller. His chair was higher than mine so that he had to look down at me—purposely, I was sure—and the way the walls closed in made me feel both on edge and defensive.

"I didn't buy them," I said, excuses coming to my lips without willing them. "I found them. Someone must have left them. The lighter too. I only had that one cigarette. I'm not even a smoker. I just wanted to try it. No big deal. Send me to detention. I won't do it again."

"You *found* them?" He was obviously skeptical. "Is that the story you're sticking with?"

"Yes, sir."

He leaned forward, putting his elbows on the desk in front of him. "Let's cut the crap, Cade. We both know these cigarettes belong to Birch."

I hesitated, wondering if it was a trap to get me to narc, then settled on something I hoped wasn't too incriminating. "You think they were his?"

"I said to cut the crap."

My mouth clamped shut. I refused to rat anyone out.

"You want to know why you're in here instead of him, don't you? Go ahead and ask."

Him telling me to do a thing made me less want to do the thing, but I was starting to realize that he might actually have the power he was so intent on making me believe he had. "Um. If you think these belong to Birch, why am I here instead of him?"

He soured at my attempt to twist his instructions, but he let it slip by without remarking. "Antoine Birch is a serial troublemaker. He will spend this year in and out of detention, and each time I'll call his parents to inform them, and each time they will dismiss his actions with some version of the *boys will be boys* refrain. It's their prerogative to blow it off. All they care is that their son graduates and makes it into Harvard, where he will study medicine and eventually become a renowned doctor. His legacy will speak well for Stark Academy, so why should I feel motivated to correct the kid for being on the path that will most please everyone?"

"You shouldn't, I guess." Unless he cared about *being* an educator that deserved respect instead of just getting by as one, but apparently he didn't.

"That's right. I shouldn't. It's a waste of my time and energy." He brought his hands together in front of him with a clap. "You, on the other hand, stand to harm me much more with your offensive actions than Antoine Birch does. If you're allowed to get by with even a minor infraction, what sort of effect would that have on the student body? What if word got out to their parents? Can you imagine what people would say if it was reported that I couldn't manage the behavior of my own stepson? How many would whisper nepotism behind our backs? Have you thought of that?"

"No, sir." But I suddenly had a feeling that Julianna

had thought about it. Or been told to think about it. Probably several times over her life.

Maybe labeling her a goody-goody had been unfair. She likely hadn't had a choice.

"Precisely. You hadn't thought of it. Which is why you are here in my office instead of Antoine Birch, because it is you that most requires to be taught a lesson, and acting as both your headmaster as well as your father, it is my duty to deliver that instruction."

"You are *not* my father," I said, probably more boldly than I should have.

"I'm the closest thing you'll ever get, and considering who you are and where you come from, you should consider it an honor to be my son. Place your hand on the desk in front of you, facing up."

A slap on the wrist, then—or palm, rather. With a ruler, most likely. It would sting, and it would be over, and I could go to class and forget the asshole shit he'd said and keep my head down for the rest of the year until I was free to get out of here.

Or I could continue to argue.

I wasn't sure if it was because I was smart or because I was scared, but backing down seemed to be the better option.

With a sigh, I placed my hand out on the desk in front of me.

Stark then picked up the pack of cigarettes and placed it in my hand.

"Sir?" I asked, unsure what he wanted from me.

"How many cigarettes are in there? Count them."

I remembered how many had been missing when I'd taken one out earlier, but I opened it and looked anyway. "Sixteen."

Next he handed me the lighter. "Smoke them."

Now I was definitely confused. "You want me to smoke one? Here? Now?"

"I want you to smoke them all."

It took me a minute, then I laughed. "You're messing with me. Funny. You had me there."

"I'm completely serious, Cade."

"You want me to smoke all of the cigarettes in here. All sixteen."

"Not at once, of course. One at a time." He leaned back in his chair. "Better get started. We're going to be here a while as it is."

I paused, still not sure. What if it was a trap? He wanted to see if I'd really do it, and then...

And then what? I was already in trouble. He didn't need to catch me in more. Was he trying to turn it into a joke? So that later he could tell my mother, *You should have seen him. He actually believed I wanted him to smoke sixteen cigarettes in a row.*

Or he really meant to teach a practical lesson—make me smoke a couple, and then when I was jittery and buzzed and feeling gross, he'd call it good, hoping it would turn me off from the damn things for good.

He was waiting. Only way to find out his intent was to light up.

It took seven minutes to smoke the first one. I watched the clock on the shelf behind him, the seconds ticking by at a snail's pace. When the ash started to fall from my cigarette, he dumped the change from a glass bowl on his desk and told me to use that.

He didn't speak again until I'd put the butt out. "Another."

I lit up again, already feeling lightheaded. I managed to smoke that one in just over six minutes. When he nodded, I lit the next one.

Halfway through the third, I'd reached my limit. "Okay. I get it. Smoking is bad." I rubbed the cigarette out in the glass bowl. "Thank you for the lesson. I won't smoke anymore."

"I told you to smoke all sixteen."

"Right. I get what you're trying to prove."

"I'm not trying to prove anything, Cade. Pick up the goddamn cigarette, and put it between your lips."

I stared at him. There wasn't a hint of amusement anywhere in his expression.

My stomach tightened. "I can't smoke anymore. I'm already feeling sick."

"Should have thought of that earlier. Light up."

"Look." I wiped my sweaty palms on my uniform khakis. "I can't. If you want to punish me another way..."

He stood up immediately. "Put both your hands on the desk in front of you. Palms up."

So now the ruler would come.

But when he stood and opened the drawer he'd unlocked earlier, he didn't pull out a ruler—he pulled out a long, black, skinny-tailed whip.

My breath caught in my ribs. Instinctively, my hands

curled back toward me as he came around the desk to stand in striking position. The spark I'd seen in his eyes before was back. "Hands open, Cade. Now."

I looked at the door behind me, wondering what would happen if I just got up and left.

"Try it and find out," he said, reading my mind.

It would catch up with me eventually, this punishment. I couldn't escape the man. He slept under the same roof I did.

Tentatively, I laid my hands out and closed my eyes so I didn't see the whip as it lashed through the air.

But, fuck, did I feel it.

My eyes flew open, and I wasn't surprised to see bloody stripes along both palms. The sting was incredible. It was the kind of pain that lingered. The kind that I knew would take at least a week before it healed.

I reached for a Kleenex on his desk and dabbed delicately at the wounds. A whip. Was that legal for an educator? Was that even legal for a stepparent?

"Still prefer the whip to the cigarettes?"

"A little late to change my mind now it's done." But given the choice again, I wasn't sure I wouldn't pick the smoking.

"Oh, we're not done. You have thirteen and a half unfinished cigarettes. Either you smoke all of them, or you get thirteen more lashes. Your choice."

My head snapped toward him. "You're kidding, right?"

"I don't kid. Choose. Personally, I'm hoping you go with the whip. It will be the messier option, but it will be

over quickly, and my office won't reek like an ashtray."
He didn't hide his smile. The prick was enjoying this.
"Choose."

I should have been angry, and I was. But more than
that, I felt trapped. Trapped like I'd never felt before,
and not just trapped between two options, but trapped
in this life—*his* life. In his *school*. In his *house*. In his
*family*.

He said he wanted me to make a choice, but he was
actually pointing out that I didn't *have* a choice. Not
really. He'd win, and I'd lose. There was nothing I could
choose to make that end another way.

My hand shaking, I picked up the lighter. I wouldn't
withstand fourteen lashes. And if I was going to lose, at
least I'd make him waste a good portion of his afternoon
on it.

It took almost two hours to smoke the rest of the
pack.

I tried to take longer, dragging out each puff,
delaying longer before I brought it to my lips again, but
Stark watched me carefully and waved the whip threat-
eningly every time I slowed down or didn't take a real
inhalation.

I threw up after the eighth cigarette. He kicked his
wastebasket toward me as soon as he realized I was going
to heave. I threw up again after the twelfth, and still he
made me finish the last one as well as the other half of
the one I'd abandoned.

And through it all, he watched me with fascination.
I'd never had someone's focus for so long. Never felt so

intensely scrutinized. Never understood the real meaning of helplessness.

Finally, when all sixteen of the cigarettes were butts in the glass bowl, my punishment was finished. Without a word, Stark dumped the ashes in the wastebasket along with the empty pack and pocketed the lighter.

"Empty the trash on your way out," he said, pulling a file off a stack and opening it up, his attention now fully on work. He didn't spare me another glance. He was done with me. He'd moved on.

I stared at him, my head pounding, my body shaking, my stomach threatening to retch again, even though I'd emptied it completely.

Then, because he'd proven his point—that he was the one in control, and I had no say—I pulled the trash bag from the can and took it with me when I left.

# FIVE

## CADE

THERE WAS STILL one more class on my schedule, but I skipped it. I wouldn't have made it through the lesson, even if I'd wanted to. Just crossing the half mile to get to our house had felt like an achievement. I'd had to stop several times, my head pounding so hard I thought it would explode, my stomach churning like there was still something in it left to expel.

When the walking path made its final curve leading to our yard, I almost collapsed in relief. I'd never thought I'd be so thankful to see that damn front porch.

Even more reason to be thankful was the sight of my mother on her knees, weeding the flowerbeds in front of the house. We'd remained at odds since my arrival, but like the little boy I'd once been who sought her out to kiss away my boo-boos, she was exactly the person I needed now.

She stood when she saw me, bringing a glove-clad

hand up to shield her eyes from the sun. "Cade? School's not over. Why are you home early?"

Then I was close enough for her to see me better, or the sun moved, because her hand fell, and her eyes grew wide. "What's wrong?" she asked, closing the distance between us. "You look terrible. Did something happen?"

I responded by bending over, my hands on my thighs, and retched in her petunias. They were pretty much dead, anyway.

"Oh, honey, are you sick?"

I felt too awful to give her a snide response—obviously, I was sick—and too grateful for the garden apron she handed me to wipe my mouth.

When I was upright again, she stepped closer, wrapping her arms around me while she pressed her lips to my forehead. "You're not warm. What's that smell?" Her nose wrinkled as she got a good inhale.

Immediately, she stepped away, her brief demonstration of compassion already over. "God, you smell like a smoking lounge on a Friday night. Was it just tobacco, or were you messing with marijuana? That stuff can be laced, you know. You have no idea if you're getting straight plant or if it's got some PCP, and if you're getting drugs from someone on campus, you need to let Langdon—"

I cut her off. "Langdon is the reason I smell like this." It was the first time I'd spoken since I'd left his office, and damn did I need a glass of water. My throat was on fire.

I crossed to the spout on the front of the house and

turned it on, then cupped my hands to bring water to my mouth.

"Don't be cryptic, Cade. What are you talking about?" Annoyance was heavy in her tone.

I drank a little more, careful not to drink too much in fear of another bout of nausea, then turned the spout off and turned to her. "I'm talking about your husband. He's a monster. He made me sit in his office and smoke an entire pack of cigarettes. That's why I look like shit. That's why I'm puking in your flowers."

She visibly rolled her eyes. "I'm really not in the mood for whatever this—"

Angrily, I cut her off. "*You're* not in the mood? Do you think *I'm* in the mood to feel like this?"

"If you're messing around with cigarettes, then I'm sorry, but you get what you deserve."

"This wasn't me, Mom. Would you listen to me for half a second? Really listen?" I waited until she gave me her full attention. "Your husband—my headmaster—sat me down in his office for two hours with a pack of cigarettes and then made me smoke every single one of them." I spoke slowly, spelling it out to her like she was a child.

Finally, she seemed to process what I was saying.

Or at least tried to process. "What do you mean *made* you? You can't force someone to—"

"You can if you threaten them. Look." I'd almost forgotten about the stripe on my palms, too distracted by the effects of chain smoking. I showed her now. "This is from a whip he keeps in his office." I only now thought to question why he had it. What he used it for. Who he used it on. "He threatened to give me more lashes if I didn't smoke them all."

She took off her garden gloves and tossed them to the ground before reaching for my right hand. Then my left. Concern marked her features as she examined the marks, though I could sense she was still wary. "You didn't do this to yourself?"

"How could I do this to myself?"

"You didn't have a friend do this?"

"Why would I have a friend do this to me?"

"Because you want to make your stepfather into the bad guy. You wanted to frame him or something."

I was growing impatient. I'd come home intent on telling my mother right away what had happened. I didn't think I'd have to convince her it was true.

Still, I knew screaming at her wouldn't get me anywhere, so I took a deep breath and tried to remain calm. "I'm not trying to frame him, Mom, or make him a bad guy. I'm trying to tell you that he *is* a bad guy. I swear on my life, this was him."

She dropped my hands and hugged herself, as though she was the one who needed the comfort. As though finding out her new husband wasn't the knight in shining armor she wanted him to be would completely alter her world.

I supposed she wasn't wrong about that.

"Why? Why would he do something like this?" It no longer sounded like skepticism but an attempt to grapple with what I was telling her.

I'd spent the whole time in his office asking myself the same thing. "I don't know. He's cruel, I think. I think he liked punishing me."

I couldn't get the image of the gleeful way he'd looked at me while I suffered out of my head. He'd definitely enjoyed it. Thinking about it made me feel sick again. And small. And embarrassed for some reason that I couldn't explain.

"Why was he punishing you? Did you do something?"

"Well, I mean." I considered lying, then thought better of it. "Yes. I did something. He caught me smoking—"

"You said he *made* you smoke."

"He did! Not the first one, though. I was out with some of the guys, okay? It was just one cigarette. I bummed it from another kid. Stark caught us, and even though the cigarettes weren't mine, I'm the only one he took to his office. And then he spent the next two hours forcing me to smoke the rest of the pack. Sixteen cigarettes, Mom. One after another. No break."

"Oh, Cade." She let out another sigh, her head shaking as she dropped her arms to her side. "He was teaching you a lesson."

My heartbeat felt heavy. I was losing her. "That wasn't what that was."

"He was. He was teaching you a lesson about smoking."

"He was *torturing* a minor."

"You're so dramatic. It was a punishment with a

moral. And, yes, punishments are uncomfortable. That's the whole point of them." She bent to pick up the apron I'd dropped and her discarded gloves, clearly having made her assessment of the situation and ready to move on.

I followed after her as she cleaned up. "This goes beyond uncomfortable, Mom. I'm pretty sure it's not even legal."

"It's extreme, yes. But sometimes extremism is called for. He's trying to teach you why smoking is bad. You haven't had a father in your life, so I can see why this sort of parental guidance could come as a shock, but honestly, you need this. This is exactly the kind of discipline you've been lacking."

I might not have ever had a father, but after a year observing Mr. Goodie with his children, I'd seen what responsible parenting looked like, and this was not it.

But that wasn't the part of her lecture that struck a nerve. "How do you even know what the fuck I need?" Her head snapped back toward me, her expression disapproving, but I wasn't going to apologize for my language or my outburst. "You abandoned me. For a year. How could you possibly have any idea that I need discipline?"

"I know by your own admission that you were caught smoking, so don't even try to play innocent with me."

"Fine! I was smoking, and I'm evil, and I deserve harsh and unusual punishments to put me in line. Is that what you want to hear?"

"What I want is a little gratitude."

"Gratitude." I repeated the word, as if I'd be less shocked hearing it from my own lips. "Unbelievable."

"Oh my God, Cade, please. Stop." She turned toward me, her body sagging with a weariness that was almost disturbing. "You've only been here three weeks, and I'm exhausted. And you can't even give this place a chance." Her voice dropped, low and convicted. "This is the best we've had it; do you realize that? You have one year to get through. One year, and this is the best chance you have for a future. This home is the best opportunity I've ever given you. Ever given *us*. So fine. Go ahead and ruin it for yourself, but you're on your own with that. You aren't going to ruin it for me."

I took a step backward, stunned by her words. Feeling them as what they were—another abandonment. Another betrayal.

Another step back, and this time I bumped into a body.

I turned in time to catch Julianna before she fell. "Sorry," she said, as if she'd been the one to bump into me. "I was trying to slip by without interrupting."

Her eyes stuck on mine, and I could feel my skin heat. Had she heard what we'd been talking about? I hoped she hadn't. Not because I cared if I'd destroyed her thoughts about her dear old dad, but because of that odd embarrassed element. There was something humiliating about being punished. About being weak enough to be punishable.

As little as I thought about my stepsister, I didn't like the idea of her finding me weak.

I definitely didn't like the weird, warm way it felt to touch her. As soon as I was sure she was upright on her own, I let her go, shoving my wounded hands in my pockets.

"You're fine, honey," my mother said, stepping around me, her voice full of cheer that hadn't been there a moment before. "We were just... Oh, look at this mess in your way." She bent to pick up the trowel she'd left on the ground and her gardening pillow. "I didn't realize how late it had gotten. I should be cleaning up and starting dinner."

She was terrible at a subject change, but Julianna followed her with it. "Um, about that... It's Dad's night in Hartford."

"Oh, that's right. The Council for Northeast Private Educators." Her expression eased with the reminder, and the cheer in her voice now sounded much more authentic. "Well, that changes things. Should we order pizza, or I could do grilled cheese?"

Julianna bit her lip, and I tried not to stare. "Actually, I was hoping I could go to my study group again. It was really helpful last time. I can grab dinner with them."

"Yes, yes. Of course," my mother said, and I could practically hear the wink-wink in her tone. "You'll be back before...?"

"He won't even know I was gone," Julianna said, then scampered into the house, closing the screen door softly behind her.

Under other circumstances, I would have tried to analyze it more—the conspiratorial interaction, the relief my mother had at a night off from her spouse, the knowledge that little-miss-perfect Juliana took advantage of her father's absence.

But I was too consumed with my own feelings. The words my mother had uttered before Julianna had shown up echoed in my mind. *You're on your own. You're on your own.*

"Do *you* have a dinner preference?" my mother asked when we were alone again, as though everything between us was fine and dandy.

Like hell was I playing that game. "I'm on my own, remember? Looks like you are too." I followed Julianna into the house, but when I went in, I let the screen door slam.

# SIX

## CADE

I SLEPT the rest of the afternoon and into the evening. When I woke up around nine, there was a plate with two cold grilled cheese sandwiches on my nightstand and a can of Coke. Sugary drinks weren't allowed in Stark's household, so I had a feeling it was meant to be an offering, but I was still too pissed to accept it.

The sandwich, though, I appreciated.

I still had the headache from earlier, but my stomach had calmed enough to want food, even cold. After inhaling the first one, I slowed down on the second, taking a bite of it then crossing to look out at the front yard as I continued to nibble.

As much time as I'd spent in my room over the last month—mostly trying to catch up from my late start to the school year—I hadn't explored the window. There was no screen, I noticed now, and the roof over the porch extended seven or eight inches underneath.

Holding the sandwich between my teeth, I opened the window. It was only about a three-foot drop to the roof. Four at most. I could easily get out, and it wouldn't be that hard to get back in.

As badly as I wanted an escape from my life, this small discovery felt enormous.

After grabbing a hoodie from my dresser, I sat down on the sill, swung my legs out over the extension, and dropped. Easy.

Instantly, I had my own hideout. *Fuckin' A.*

I crawled more to the center of the roof then sat down, brought my knees to my chest, and finished my sandwich. It was chilly, and I was glad I'd donned the extra layer, but beyond that the night was clear and peaceful. The stars were out. The moon, bright behind the treetops. The only sounds were of the crickets and the occasional hoot of an owl and the rustle of a breeze through the trees.

Then something that sounded husky. A tortured moan.

What?

I listened. Waited to hear it again. Less than a minute later, I did.

No, that wasn't a *tortured* moan. It was an *aroused* moan.

I crept toward the edge of the porch roof and looked for the source, finding it quickly—two figures sitting on the metal garden bench my mother had placed two weekends ago at the side of the drive near the bird bath.

Well, one figure sitting, the other kneeling with its head over the other's lap, the shadows of the night making it impossible to make out either person's identity.

*Who the fuck...?*

The moon peeked up over the canopy then, shining light on the yard. Antoine Birch was the figure sitting, his head thrown back in pleasure.

And even though I couldn't see her face, the figure bobbing up and down over Birch's exposed cock seemed to have the shape of Julianna.

Then he wasn't talking horseshit earlier about her reputation.

It was startling. But I felt more than surprised. I felt...

I didn't know what I felt, exactly. My chest burned and my breath felt shallow, and I didn't want to be watching, but I couldn't force myself to look away.

If I had to put a name to the emotion, it was anger.

Except I wasn't quite sure whom I was angry with. Or why. Or what to do about it.

So I just kept watching, finishing my sandwich in angry bites despite having lost my appetite. And a few minutes later, when Birch's body got rigid and his moan elongated, I kept watching as she sat back on her knees and wiped the back of her hand over her mouth, apparently having swallowed.

Lucky Birch.

No, not lucky Birch. This was my stepsister. A girl I barely knew, but my stepsister nonetheless. There was no fucking way I was going to think about her like *that*.

But I was definitely thinking about her. More than I had before. Wondering how I'd been so wrong about who she was. Curious about what other surprises she might have in store, and if there was anything to learn that might be useful. Or illuminating.

I continued to watch as they chatted afterward, their voices too low to make out. There was no cuddling or kissing or anything to suggest the act had been romantic, and Birch didn't make any move to reciprocate. Prick. Eventually, he pulled out a pack of smokes and lit a cigarette which he ended up sharing with her.

Strangely, that seemed even more intimate than the blow job.

Also strange was how I was suddenly jonesing for a smoke myself despite how terrible I'd felt all day. *Great lesson, Langdon. All you got me was hooked, asshole.*

When the cigarette was burned down to a butt, the two stood up, and I crept back away from the edge, returning to my seclusion and my thoughts. Thoughts now centered less on my mother and the man she'd married and more on the other member of our household.

My solitude didn't last long after that.

"Oh, wow. This is really high," Julianna said, her voice behind me.

Startled, my head flew to my window where she was perched cautiously on the sill, peering down at the ground, obviously anxious about the distance.

I was equally anxious, but not about the height. *What the fuck was she doing in my room?*

"You're lucky," she continued, making herself comfortable. "My window doesn't have access to the roof like this. If it did, I'd probably be too scared to climb out." She shivered.

"It's not really that..." I was distracted by the length of her neck as she tilted it up to look at the sky. I hadn't realized how pretty her throat was. Or that women could have pretty throats. "What do you want?" I snapped, suddenly irritated.

She shrugged. "Just wanted to know if you enjoyed the show."

It took me a beat to get what she was referring to. "If you don't want to be watched, maybe don't do your thing in public."

"Not really many options around here."

"I guess not."

She didn't say anything after that, and I tried to ignore her. Tried to pretend she wasn't there, breathing the same night air, sharing in my escape.

But even silent, even not looking at her, she was still *there*. Present. With me.

"Brought you something," she said after an eternity had passed. "Though, after this afternoon, maybe you don't want them."

Intrigued, I glanced back to see her waving a pack of cigarettes and a lighter.

"How did you...?" Had she overheard me and my mother talking after all? I could feel embarrassment creeping up all over again.

"Antoine told me you took the fall for him and Troy.

Figured you deserved them as a reward, but maybe you're done with them after getting caught."

So she didn't know the whole story. That was a relief.

Not willing to ignore a gift when I got so few, I crawled over until I was in reach of her. Then I stretched my hand out, my heart jumping when my finger accidentally brushed her skin as I accepted the offering.

Leaning back onto my heels, I took out a cigarette and lit it. When I tried to hand the rest back, she shook her head. "Keep them."

I shoved them in the pocket of my hoodie and kept one hand in there as I inhaled. "Are these from you or from him?"

"I asked him if I could have them. He didn't ask who they were for. I'm sure he assumed they were for me."

"Awfully nice of him to give up a whole pack. Especially when he lost one earlier." Though money wasn't an issue for him, it couldn't be easy to get smokes on a closed campus.

"Well, I'd been awfully nice to him, as you saw..."

For the briefest second, I wondered if that was the whole reason she'd sucked him off—so she could get cigarettes to give to me.

Then I realized how stupid that thought was. Not everything was about me. In fact, according to my mother, very few things were.

"Birch your boyfriend?" I knew from what he'd said earlier that they weren't together but was curious what she'd say.

She stared off in the distance. "Nah. Honestly, I

don't even think he likes me very much. He just gets off on fooling around with the headmaster's daughter."

I wanted to ask her why she did it then, but that felt too personal.

Besides, the thought of her potentially gushing over Antoine Birch made me nauseated for some reason.

Actually, it was probably just the cigarette because I certainly didn't give a flying fuck about who Julianna Stark gushed over.

Did I?

"I have something else for you too." She shook a tin of mints. "I'll leave them on your dresser. Dad doesn't have the best sense of smell, but I'm paranoid."

"Thanks," I said, not sure what to make of her kindness. Not sure what to make of her at all.

"Anytime." She stood, but she kept her head out, and I could sense she had something more to say for several beats before she spoke. "It could have been worse."

"What could have?" *Did* she know what her father had done? Was she guessing?

She ignored my question. "It *will* be worse. You're going to have to figure out how you're going to survive here or..."

"Or what?"

"Or...you just won't."

Strange advice. *Ominous* advice. I took a long draw on my cigarette, stared into the night, and tried to process all of it. This house. This situation. This girl, with her pale eyes and serious expression and lush lips.

Lips that had, less than thirty minutes before, been wrapped around another boy's cock.

When I turned back to look at her again, I was surprised to find I was disappointed that she was gone.

# SEVEN
## JOLIE

*Present*

THE HOUSE SMELLED EXACTLY the same—a combination of Lysol and home cooking—and with a single inhalation, I was swept back to the past. With Cade right behind me, it was the good memories that came first. Some of the best moments of my life were associated with him in this place.

I glanced at the hallway upstairs, halfway expecting to see the ghost of my former self peeking through the railing. The first time I'd seen him, he'd stolen my breath. How long after had he stolen my heart?

But then came the other memories—the bad memories, the complicated memories—rolling in like a tornado, intent on destroying everything in its wake. My body had prepared for it before my mind, the constant fear. My shoulders were already tense. My ears were already straining for sounds of another person in the house. Hyperawareness switched on like it was a function of my autonomic system, as much a reflex as breathing and temperature regulation. *Where was he now? Was he close? Was he coming for me?*

The fact that I didn't hear him only heightened my tension.

"The living room's new," Cade said, reminding me that it had been seventeen years since he'd last been here.

Carla followed his gaze, her forehead creased. "I guess we had that redone after you'd gone. But it's definitely not new."

"A couple of years after graduation, I think," I said.

"So sorry I couldn't be here for that." Having been groomed to not display emotions in this household, Cade's voice seemed both out of place and to be expected. It occurred to me then that this might be harder for him than for me. I hadn't been thrown out of this house—I'd left voluntarily.

And damn, it was hard for me.

Without thinking, I reached out to take his hand and gave it a comforting squeeze. Who it was meant to comfort—him or me—I didn't know. I did know I couldn't imagine being here without him.

Carla cleared her throat. "I didn't expect to see you again so soon, Julianna. Considering how upset you were when you left, I'm surprised you're back."

Cade swung his attention toward me, eagerly picking up on details I'd continually refused to give him.

And now I had to give him something. Because if I didn't, he'd ask her. "I came last month. To ask my father for some money that he promised me years ago. He said no."

Put like that, it made it seem like the reasons I wanted my father gone were money related, which wasn't exactly the case. "It's more complicated than that," I amended. "But that's the gist of it."

He studied me. "He didn't need more reasons to be hated," he said, and I let out the breath I'd been holding, afraid that he'd press for more.

"No, he didn't." I was sure this wasn't the end of it, but at least it was the end of it for now.

"It's a good surprise," Carla said, her tone at odds with the statement, her eyes pinned on our interlaced hands. "Are you staying the night?"

"No, just dropping by." I started to drop Cade's hand, her attention making me feel ill at ease, but he wouldn't let mine go, a visible demonstration of defiance.

I didn't fight him, but the connection no longer felt soothing.

"You were in the area?"

"We, um." I looked to him, hoping he'd step in. When he didn't, I tried to remember what we'd practiced in the car. "We happened to both be in New York at the same time, and we met up, which led to a trip down memory lane, and on a whim, we thought we'd come up here. See how things have changed. See what's the same."

"My idea," he said, seeming to understand that that made more sense, considering the way my last visit had ended.

"He talked me into a day trip. I have to be back at my job on Monday." That last part was a spontaneous lie. An excuse not to stay.

Not a good enough excuse, apparently. "Monday is three days away. You can stay the weekend."

"I'm sure Langford would love that," Cade muttered too quietly for Carla to hear.

I jumped in with a smile before she asked him to repeat himself. "I think dinner is all we can promise."

"Then, I'll take what I can get." An awkward beat passed. "Well. I suppose we don't need to spend all evening standing in the foyer. Come on in."

She headed toward the dining room, leading us as though we were first-time guests and not family members. "It's nothing fancy tonight. You know I don't prepare extravagant meals when your father's away, so it's just homemade soup heated up, but I'll throw some rolls in the oven, and it should be enough."

I exchanged a glance with Cade. "Dad's not here?"

She grabbed a lace tablecloth from the dining hutch as soon as we entered the room—the table wouldn't be bare at this time of day if Dad was here.

"It was a testing day at school," she said, smoothing the cloth out and tugging one side so it fell evenly. "He doesn't need to be around for that, so he left early for the weekend."

"Left for where?" Cade asked.

"The cabin. Finally cold enough for ice fishing. It's the first time this season he's been able to get up there. Your father's gotten quite passionate about the sport."

"He's not my father." His hand tensed in mine.

In contrast, I felt mine relax.

He wasn't here. I didn't have to see him. What a relief. "He'll be gone all weekend?" I asked, just to be sure before I got too comfortable.

"Be back Sunday." She stood upright, the business with the tablecloth completed. This time when she smiled, it reached her eyes. "You could stay until then."

"We really hadn't planned—"

"We'll stay," Cade said, cutting me off.

I was too taken aback to hide my shock. "We will?"

He gave a one-shoulder shrug. "Seems silly to rush back. We have our luggage."

"Good," Carla said before I could argue. "You can have your old rooms. They both still have beds in them."

"They both have locks on the outside so you can keep us apart?"

This time she heard Cade's snide remark, and her smile fell. "I wouldn't know anything about that."

"No. Of course, you wouldn't."

"Cade..." I warned. I had no idea what his intentions were, but agreeing to stay then picking a fight seemed counterproductive.

"What?"

"Play nice."

The acid remained in his expression, but he did manage something that almost looked like a smile.

"Well," Carla said, breaking through the tension. "I'll put the bread in the oven if you want to set the table. We should use the china."

"The china?" I glanced at the cabinet against the far wall. We'd only ever brought the good dishes out on holidays.

"It's a special occasion," she explained, her tone flat. "Not every day my children return home for a visit. We should celebrate." With that, she disappeared through the swinging door into the kitchen.

As soon as she was gone, Cade dropped my hand—validating my suspicion that it had been a show—and opened the china cabinet.

"Why did you say we'd stay?" I hissed, taking the plate he handed to me.

"Why would we not?"

I set the dish on the table, then took the next one he offered. "Oh, I don't know. Because we hate it here?"

"Yeah. There is that. You could throw a plate. Maybe make you feel better."

"Very funny." The set was already missing a dish, and thinking about the circumstances surrounding that sent me down a rabbit hole of emotions, which was exactly why I didn't want to be here longer than necessary. Too many complicated memories.

Cade paused, holding the last plate instead of passing it over. "Did you hear her? 'My children.' Like we were once a happy family. And what's with this whole 'we should celebrate' act?"

There had been other parts of our conversation that had sparked my interest more than this, but I considered her words now. "Maybe it's easier for her to pretend that we were."

"That's an awfully generous outlook."

It was, I supposed. And maybe I was in a better position to have it than Cade since she hadn't been my mother, and she hadn't abandoned me.

More, though, I'd come to terms with something that I wasn't sure he'd yet realized. "To be fair, she was just as much his victim as we were."

His jaw tensed. "No." He waved the plate at me, emphasizing his point. "She doesn't get to be forgiven. She was complicit."

I didn't want to argue.

I also knew these feelings of his weren't going to go away. "Can you really spend two days here? Because I really don't know that I can."

He opened his mouth, then shut it.

When he opened it again, he sighed. "Look, I know it's not what we planned, and that this is awful. Probably even more awful than it seems on the surface. But this is really a blessing in disguise. It will give us more time to find the key, and who knows? Maybe we'll find something else useful. Or get something out of *her*." He gestured toward the kitchen, indicating his mother. "We have to remember why we're here."

Oh, I hadn't forgotten. The goal was to prove my

father was involved in a sex trafficking ring or set him up for it.

"Besides, we can't go to the cabin while he's there. Might as well stay here until he's on his way back."

To succeed, we needed to get the key for the cabin safe from his home office and then use it to plant evidence, which meant my father couldn't be there. And he was right—staying here was our best chance, but that didn't uncoil the tight knot in my stomach. Even without my father present, fear remained. It was a stench soaked so deeply into the woodwork of our home that it lingered after the source was removed.

"And then we'll go to the cabin together, right?" I asked, needing confirmation that there would be something more between us before we had to be over.

Before he answered, his mother pressed through the swinging door with a crockpot full of soup in her hands. "It will be just another few minutes for the bread. Let me help you finish with the place settings."

We fell quickly into a rhythm from years ago—one of us putting out the goblets, another filling them with ice, the third following behind with a pitcher of water. The food came to the table in the same method, a practiced machine of serving, and when everything was in place—the head of the table left empty—several seconds passed before any of us dared to be the first to sit.

We'd been well trained.

It was Cade who pulled his chair out first. "Let's get at it. I'm starved."

We skipped the prayer, Cade immediately reaching

for the ladle. I followed suit and put a warm roll on my plate before passing the basket to Carla. Once everyone was served, we preoccupied ourselves with eating, minutes passing with no one talking.

It didn't take long before the silence became heavy.

So much to say. So much better left unsaid. Opening conversation felt like walking into a minefield, and none of us wanted to be the one who took the first step. Even the most innocent comment could be a trigger.

I was the first to break. "I'd forgotten how good your cooking is, Carla."

"Hard to remember when you don't visit," she said.

And there went the first bomb.

I took a slow breath in but still didn't manage to hold back what came out. "Yes, I suppose missing out on your cooking is the price for my mental health and well-being. Perhaps it was a poor life choice."

Cade chuckled across from me.

"He looked for you, you know," she said casually, as though I'd simply been misplaced. "He wouldn't admit that to you, but he did."

I took a sip of water before I responded. "I figured he would. I didn't want to be found."

She shook her head in admonition. "Broke his heart when you took off. Broke mine too. It really wasn't fair to us the way you took off. It wasn't fair to—"

Wary of how she'd finish the sentence, I cut her off. "It wasn't fair to anyone. I get it. You want to know who it was fair to? Me. It was time I looked out for myself, and so I did." I stared at her pointedly, hoping she understood the boundaries that I'd set up for the conversation.

Hoping she wouldn't try to venture past them.

Thankfully, she stayed inside the bounds. "Seems to have done good for you. The blonde is a bit extreme, but you look well."

I gritted my teeth through the backhanded compliment. "Thank you. I am well."

"I have to say," she said, lifting her spoon to gesture toward her son. "I'm surprised you didn't immediately go looking for this one."

"I didn't want to be found either," Cade said, not missing a beat.

"I know. Your father looked for you too."

He was sitting across from me, but I could feel him go rigid as clearly as if I were pressed against him. "First of all, he's not my father. Second of all, if that man was looking for me, it could not have been for any good reason."

"I mean, do you blame him? After going to court like you did. After what you did to his daughter. And then just leaving when—"

"Carla," I interrupted quickly, not sure what to say but needing her not to finish her sentence.

Cade saved me from having to come up with more. "Have you somehow forgotten that he beat me to a pulp the last time I was here? I barely walked out of here. He broke two ribs. My face was swollen for a month. And you're talking to me about blame?"

"Rebellious behavior needs extreme parenting," she

said, her volume reasonable, unlike his. "You kept pushing him and pushing him. What did you expect your father to do?"

Abruptly, he slammed his fist on the table, making his soup spill on the cloth. "He's not my goddamn father!" He stood up and threw his napkin on the table. "I've lost my appetite. I need a cigarette."

I watched Carla as she watched him storm away, looking for signs that she was upset. That had been the position I'd assumed as a teen—the peacekeeper. The comforter. The one who made sure no one else set off Daddy's temper.

Even in his absence, I found myself slipping back into the role. "It's hard to be back here."

Her eyes snapped back to mine. "You don't need to make excuses for him."

"I'm not. I'm explaining something about him. If you're looking to know your son, I thought it might help."

"So you know everything about the relationship between sons and their mothers, do you?"

"Carla... Please, don't make this bigger than what it is."

She ignored me. "And you know what's best for Cade?"

"I didn't say—"

"Is that why you haven't told him? Because you know what's best for him?"

I sat back, surprised she'd realized. Glad, too, since it would make this visit easier. Also, ashamed. Always ashamed.

"Or are you thinking about what's best for yourself?" she pressed.

I stared into my soup bowl. "You know why I haven't told him."

"Well, I wouldn't expect you to be completely honest about it. You never have been before. Why start now?"

The remark felt like a slap, but I tried not to react. It seemed like an especially bad idea since I didn't know if she actually knew the truth or if she was just referring to the truth she thought she knew.

For half a second, I considered just telling her. Considered clearing the air and putting everything on the table, and maybe I would have followed through if it were just the two of us.

But there was Cade.

And she was right—I was looking out for what was best for both of us, which meant keeping my mouth shut.

"I'm not trying to tell you what to do, Julianna," she said, her voice softer.

*It's Jolie*, I said in my head. "No, of course you're not."

"But this affects me too. What if I had said something I shouldn't?"

"You didn't. And I hope you won't. It would really mean a lot to me if you didn't."

She sat back in her chair, her expression thoughtful.

Like every other relationship in this household, my relationship with my stepmother was complex. For the most part, we'd understood each other, and when we didn't, we'd given each other grace, knowing that the things a woman did to survive weren't always easy to explain.

But that had been in the past.

We weren't the same women we'd been, and maybe her understanding had reached a limit. "He's going to find out eventually if you're going to keep up this..." She searched for the word. "This *couple* thing—"

"We're not a couple." We'd had one night together, but I wasn't stupid enough to think it meant anything. Not when he'd made it clear how angry he still was with me.

"You sure look together."

"It's temporary."

"Does he know that?"

I started to answer then got caught up in the possibility she alluded to. What if he didn't know we were fleeting? What if he wanted us to be more?

The bubble of hope quickly burst when I remembered why we could never be more. Because, as she'd just clearly pointed out, my secrets would eventually be revealed.

And this...this he could never know.

"I would have thought you would be happy to hear this was temporary," I said, swallowing past the lump in my throat.

She didn't hesitate. "I am. What the two of you are doing? It's sick. It was sick then; it's sick now. He's your brother."

And here was where *my* understanding reached its

limit. "He's not my brother," I snapped. "He was never my brother. Just like you were never my mother."

She sat up straighter, taken aback by my outburst. "Ungrateful. Both of you have always been so ungrateful."

My first instinct was to backpedal. To apologize. To smooth her ruffled feathers and make her happy. Make her pleased.

But I was tired of those old habits. Hadn't I left them behind? Wasn't that why I'd run away and changed my name, so that I could be someone different? Someone who didn't kowtow and adulate and soothe? Someone who didn't stay and stay and stay, no matter what was said or done to me?

"You know what, Carla?" I threw my napkin into my soup bowl. "I'm not hungry anymore, either."

For the first time in my life, I got up from that damn dinner table and walked away.

# EIGHT

## JOLIE

I FOUND Cade in his old bedroom, half sitting on the window frame with a lit cigarette, looking out over the front yard.

Leaning against the doorframe, I took advantage of being unnoticed and looked around. The room had been redone after he'd left years ago, and it had been redone again since I'd left. Now it seemed to function as a guest room, though I couldn't imagine who would ever visit. The walls had been painted real-estate beige, and the twin bed had been exchanged for a double with tan and gray bedding that was neither masculine nor feminine. The area rug that I'd helped pick last time was gone as well, leaving the wood floor exposed.

I tried not to make anything of the fact that my suitcase sat next to his against the dresser. Maybe he was fully intending to take mine down the hall and just hadn't gotten to it yet.

That was the scenario I should have been wanting, but a ridiculous flutter in the center of my chest said I hoped differently.

"Always the rebel," I said, ignoring my stupid, stupid heart.

He didn't startle at my presence, making me wonder how long he'd known I'd been standing there. After ashing out the cracked window, he held the pack out toward me. "Want one?"

His guilt-free smile made my stomach go topsy-turvy, and not just because his boldness made me nervous, despite my adult status and that I'd just been brave enough to leave the table downstairs. "No. I'm scared of getting caught." I shut the door, though, and crossed to him, reaching for his cigarette. "So I'll share yours instead."

He laughed, and this time my stomach did a complete flip. He'd so rarely been joyful in this house, and every time he had been, it lit me up like a firefly because his happiness was not only infectious, it belonged only to me.

It was scary how much I liked that it only belonged to me now too.

I tried to keep my head on why we were here. "Did you check out his office?"

"You didn't?" It surprised me when he shook his head. I'd thought for sure he would have done that as soon as he'd left me with his mother in the dining room.

"It was locked," he clarified. "Another good reason

we're staying the night. I can slip down there after she's gone to sleep."

It needed to be him because he knew how to pick a lock, but I was the one who knew where he kept the spare key to the cabin safe and what it looked like. "We can slip down there together."

I waited for him to protest, but he didn't.

"This is new," he said, rapping a knuckle against the glass. It had been replaced after we'd been caught together with a window that only cranked open a few inches. "No late-night sneaking across the roof now. Yours got switched out too?"

"Naturally." I took a drag from the cigarette and blew it out the opening, watching the smoke mix with my breath in the cold air. "Except he didn't realize about the one in my bathroom."

His grin turned sly. "Too bad it's so cold. We could climb out for old time's sake."

It was a dizzying thought—going out on the roof always had my head spinning because of the height, but it was more than that. Recapturing even a sliver of that part of our lives was tempting. He'd been the most irresistible of drugs. A stimulant and an opioid all in one. One small hit, and I'd be paradoxically both soaring and numb.

But then I'd want more and more and more.

There was no more addictive escape than Cade Warren.

Was that really such a sin? Wanting to feel good?

Finding pleasure and taking it? Finding love and holding it close?

Carla's accusations from earlier clung to me, and despite knowing better than to let her get to me, she'd gotten into my head. "Do you think we were *wrong?*" I asked when I handed back the cigarette.

He looked at me quizzically as he took a drag. "For us?"

"We were related."

"We weren't related."

"Related by marriage. We lived together."

"So?" He offered me the cigarette again, and when I shook my head, he tossed it out the window.

"So it's taboo."

That devious grin returned. "It's hot."

Unexpected arousal trickled between my thighs. He'd never acted like the wrongness of our situation had been a turn-on. "Yeah?"

"You're hot."

My breath caught as he wrapped an arm around me and drew me to him, standing up at the same time. My body flush against his, I could feel exactly how hot he thought it was. How hot he thought *I* was.

"It's funny," he said, his finger gliding along my collarbone, hidden beneath my sweater. "I thought you were hot *despite* being my stepsister back then. Now, being my stepsister might be part of what makes you so sexy."

His finger continued down, down, down. To my breast and tickled over my peaked nipple, drawing a gasp from me before he bent closer and danced his mouth over mine. "So. Fucking. Sexy."

The taunting made me insane, and I thought I'd die when he only brushed his mouth against my eager lips. Once, twice. I was on fire when he finally let me have his kiss, and though it had only been hours since he'd had his mouth on mine, it again felt new, like something I hadn't had in years. Decades.

It was intoxicating the way his lips pulled gently at mine, tugging and teasing before growing greedy, and the kiss turned sinful, his tongue giving an explicit demonstration of how deeply he wanted other parts of him to be buried inside of me. I gasped again when his hands slid inside my jeans and panties to grab my ass, and he hauled me against the rigid bar at my belly.

"I wasn't sure we were doing this again." It was true, but in the moment, I couldn't imagine the possibility of *not* doing it, and what I really meant was a warning for myself. *You really shouldn't be doing this again.*

It was a warning I had no plans to heed.

He nibbled along my jaw until his mouth was near my ear. "I hope that's not a problem because I really have to fuck you."

"I think I really need to be fucked." The words dissolved into a whimper as he pushed a long finger inside me and discovered how wet I was.

"Oh, baby, you do. You really, really do."

I spread my legs wider, inviting his finger to probe me deeper, even though the angle wasn't the best, and my jeans were restricting, and what I desperately wanted was much wider than his single finger. He humored me —or tormented me, depending on how I wanted to look at it—for a bit, kissing me and fingering me until I paid him back for the torture by rubbing my palm over the granite bulge in the front of his pants.

Abruptly, he broke away, and I was somewhat satisfied to find him breathing as heavily as I was.

Barely three seconds passed before he tore off his pullover and then reached for the bottom of my sweater to draw it over my head. He tossed it to the ground then palmed my breasts while I worked on unfastening his button-down.

"We never got to fuck in this room." He tweaked both my nipples at once, and I shivered from the jolt of pleasure-pain.

"There was that hand job that one Sunday." His shirt was finally open, and I paused to kiss the eagle tattoo across his chest. "When Daddy was at the cabin, and Carla was taking a nap."

"You kept stopping to listen because you swore you'd heard something."

"That must have been the worst hand job."

"The torture made me so fucking hot." He reached behind me to unclasp my bra. Once he'd freed my breasts, he gathered them in his hands, bringing me with him as he walked backward. When the back of his legs hit the bed, he sat down. Then he spent the next several minutes adoring my flesh with his tongue and teeth and hands.

"You were never this hot," he said after teasing one nipple to a swollen point. "And you were hot."

"You're misremembering."

"You were branded in my memory hot. I'm not misremembering anything."

My chest squeezed at his subtext—*I never forgot you. I never moved on.*

I knew it to be true without him saying it. Knew it as profoundly as I knew that I hadn't gotten over him, and the ramifications of that honesty ached so much that I pulled away with the noble intent of putting an end to this before we were further consumed by this desire.

But as soon as I was out of his arms, I knew the only place I was going was back in them.

"I got something when we stopped for gas," I said, giving a reason for my retreat by going to my bag and pulling out the box I'd purchased while he'd been in the bathroom.

He raised an inquisitive brow. "You didn't think we were still doing this, and yet you have condoms?"

"I'd hoped we would."

He reached into his back pocket and pulled out three single condoms, the kind that looked like they'd come from a restroom dispenser. "I'd decided we would." He stood just long enough to toe off his shoes and finish undressing. "Get naked, and get over here."

I stripped as quickly as I could, then grabbed a condom and straddled his lap. I'd never straddled him like this, never been the one to sheathe him, and yet there was a strange sense of déjà vu as I unrolled the latex over his length.

I might not have ever lived this, but I'd imagined it. Imagined it in detail. Imagined it happening in this room, in a smaller bed. Imagined it while...

Just before I climbed onto him, I was hit with a sudden memory. "You fucked Amelia in here."

It was a statement because in my gut I was sure, but it was also a question since I'd never gotten him to confirm.

Seventeen years later, his mouth split into a guilty grin. "I did. I did."

"I knew it!" That fucker. "I was so jealous."

"Get on my cock, and then you can tell me." He was already guiding me over his jutting erection, so all I had to do was sink down, and he was filling me.

"So, so jealous." I bit my lip, the sudden intrusion of him dominating all other thoughts and sensations. It felt like I was being stretched past my limit, not just physically but mentally. Emotionally too. Every part of me going taut as he pushed his way inside me.

"So jealous," he repeated. "I like you jealous."

I was still adjusting to him when he clamped his hands on my hips and tilted me forward, coaxing me to move.

At his urging, I lifted myself up an inch, then dropped back down. Then repeated the motion, forcing myself to ride him when a part of me wanted to simply sit still and feel him twitching inside of me.

"Yes, do that," he encouraged. "Bounce on my cock,

just like that." He helped me, digging his fingers into my skin as he lifted me up and down, setting a rapid tempo.

"Did you listen at the door?" he asked, his eyes pinned to where we were joined. "Did you hear how hard she was trying to be quiet?"

Did he really remember that? It made my stomach burn to think that he did, but lower, my belly felt tight, and my pussy tingled.

And to be fair, I remembered distinctly what I'd been doing, and it hadn't been listening at the door. "I laid on my bed and pretended I was her."

His eyes flew up to mine. "Fuck, are you serious? Did you fuck yourself with your fingers and imagine it was me?"

"Yes."

He groaned, and I swore he got thicker inside of me. "What part of me did you think about? My fingers or my cock?"

Probably both, though I couldn't remember for sure.

But my uninformed fantasies were not as interesting as what had been happening in this room at the same time. Certainly not as interesting as the way my core pulsed when I thought about what he'd done with her. "You tell me, Cade."

Abruptly, he flipped me over so that I was on the bed, my legs wrapped around his waist, and he was bent over me. "You want to know what I did with Amelia?" His thrusts were slow and shallow. "Really?"

"I do." I lifted my ass, wanting him deeper, but he held my hips in place and refused to give me all of him.

"We kept our clothes on," he said, pausing to lick across my nipple. "We were wearing our school uniforms, so I got her panties off her." Another pause, another swipe of his tongue. "She had that little school skirt on, which made her cunt easy to access."

My pussy clenched with his coarse words.

"Then I pulled her onto my lap." He kissed me. "And turned her around. Because when she wasn't facing me, I could pretend the pussy riding my cock belonged to you."

He shoved all the way inside of me, drawing a whimper out of my mouth that he swallowed with a rough kiss. His mouth stayed locked to mine as he found a new torturous tempo. The bed squeaked, the headboard thumped against the wall, and while a part of me worried Carla would hear downstairs, another part of me was sorry the whole school wouldn't hear, and I urged him on.

"Faster," I pleaded against his lips. "Deeper. More."

He gave what I asked for, his pelvis rubbing against me in just the right way. Combined with the insanely erotic talk, I could feel an orgasm building, even without clitoral stimulation.

He was aware of me, could feel me tensing around him. "Don't come," he said sharply, his rhythm unfaltering.

I couldn't stop it. Especially now that he'd uttered the command, I was definitely going to come.

"Do not come, Jolie."

"I need to come," I begged.

"Don't. Don't do it. You should be as tortured as you made me that day with that hand job."

I couldn't stop it. I was on the edge.

"You should be as tortured as you made me every day that I spent in this house, thinking of you sleeping in a room down the hall. You should be as tortured as you made me every time I heard your shower go on, and I had to beat off in my hand while I pictured you naked under the water. Do you feel that tortured yet?"

If he only knew.

If he only knew how tortured I'd been then. How tortured I was now. How tortured I'd been all the years we'd spent apart, and I'd fantasized of only him.

I couldn't keep on being tortured. I wouldn't last. I couldn't...

I burst suddenly, like a rainstorm on a summer's day, heat and sensation flooding over me in a giant wave. My vision dissolved into several black spots. My limbs quivered, and pleasure invaded me as every nerve ending in my body pulsed like the heavy beat at a dance club.

"Oh, you're going to come all over my cock? You're going to make a big mess all over it?" Cade pushed through my tightened opening, and I could tell from his ragged voice he wasn't far from letting go himself. "Who said you could do that? Huh? Who said you could?" The last words came out gritted as his body tensed and sputtered before he collapsed on the bed.

He recovered before I did. My breathing still uneven and my heart still racing, he pulled me to my side to face him and anchored an arm at my waist.

Then he kissed me. Slow and deep and tender.

When he pulled back, he brought his hand to my cheek. "I can give you money, Jolie. No matter how much you need. More than your father ever promised you. I won't even miss it."

I'd hoped he would forget that exchange. I'd known he'd take it as a reason for why I'd come to him, and he wasn't wrong.

He just wasn't exactly right, either.

"It's not about the money." I brought my knuckles up to brush along the short hair along his jaw to let him know I appreciated the offer. "It's about..." I trailed off, not sure how to explain without telling him all of it.

Even then, I wasn't sure he'd understand.

Then again, maybe he was the only one who actually could.

"It's about everything he ever did to us," I said, giving it my best shot. "To all of us. Every pain and ache he caused. Every happiness he denied. And then fuck him for taking this too."

I didn't realize the tear that slipped until Cade was wiping it away with a gentle press of his lips. "We're going to destroy him, Jolie. I promise. We'll get him."

I believed him.

I only worried who else would be destroyed along the way.

# NINE
## CADE

*Past*

AMELIA SAW me as soon as I entered the library. "What happened?" she whisper-asked after throwing her arms around me in a blatant display of affection. "Did you get detention? Are you still going to be able to go on the New York City trip?"

She knew I'd just come from Stark's office—in trouble this time for walking on the lawn, which was dumb because *everyone* walked on the lawn without repercussions, not to mention that it was November, and we'd already had our first snowfall, and all the grass was dead.

But I'd become a target for the headmaster. I wasn't the only student he singled out, definitely wasn't the only one who got sent to his office, but when I'd compared my punishments to other kids, there was definitely a discrepancy. Birch usually got sent to detention for his stunts. Troy would be assigned extra papers. Alice Erickson had been scolded for not wearing an appropriate uniform and sent to her room to change.

No one I'd talked to had ever received physical discipline. No one else had been made to smoke entire packs of cigarettes or been struck with a yardstick along the back of their thighs or been locked in a cramped cupboard for several hours.

Today, I'd been forced to drink three 24-ounce bottles of water over three hours without being allowed to go to the bathroom. He hadn't stayed with me the whole time, thank God, but he'd strapped me to the chair so I couldn't leave. I'd considered urinating all over myself just to piss him off, but experience had told me that would only end up making the situation worse for myself.

I'd just gotten to the point where relieving myself was no longer a choice when he'd let me go.

I wasn't going to admit that to Amelia. It was too embarrassing. It made me feel weak. And what if she was like my mother and didn't believe me?

It was much easier to lie about my visits to his office.

"Just a talking to," I whispered after giving her a brief kiss. "You know how he is. He thinks he has to make examples of bad behavior or else no one will think he's doing his job."

"You have such a good attitude." She leaned in to kiss me again.

"Amelia Lu," Ms. Coates' voice cut sharply across the quiet library. "Study hall means study, not make-out sessions with your boyfriend."

"He's not my boyfriend," she muttered with an eye roll as she disentangled herself from me. Louder she said, "Sorry, Ms. Coates."

"And where are you supposed to be, Mr. Warren?"

"Mr. Garner sent me for a reference book," I lied. I was supposed to be in Physics with Ms. Ruiz, and I couldn't imagine a scenario where she'd send me to the library for a book during class.

"Better get to it then," Ms. Coates said before turning her attention to another student who had a question about the internet restrictions.

"I'll talk to you later," I promised Amelia, squeezing her ass quickly before letting her get back to her studying. She was a sweet girl—too sweet for me to be messing around with, probably, but she'd been the one to pursue me. When I'd told her I was only interested in a physical relationship, she'd shrugged her shoulders, got down on her knees, and sucked me off right then.

Who was I to question her ability to stay casual?

Okay, I knew there was potential to break her heart in the end; another Heather Price situation that would likely blow up in my face eventually. Her "he's not my boyfriend" statement had been made for my benefit, because she certainly acted like she thought I was her boyfriend most of the time, which was exactly why I should have been running in the other direction.

But doing the right thing with Amelia was hardly on my priority list. I didn't have the bandwidth for such nobility. School was harder than I was used to. Living in the Stark household was practically like living in a prison, and with him constantly on my ass, sex had been a welcome stress reliever.

After today, though, I needed more than an escape. I was worked up enough to seek an action plan. Since I had zero power in this situation, I needed an ally, and while I wasn't ready to share the truth with Amelia—she wasn't really in a position to help anyway—there was someone who I was pretty sure had some insight, and she had study hall right now too.

I found Julianna in a quiet corner of the library, alone at a circular table with several schoolbooks spread out in front of her, the picture-perfect student.

Except that instead of studying, she was wrapped up in a women's magazine.

It had to have been borrowed. Her father didn't approve of any reading that wasn't highbrow literature. She wasn't allowed much television viewing either, and the guy was so insane about her study habits that he sometimes bolted her in her room with a lock on the outside.

Because Stark was so controlling of her free time—and to an extent, mine as well—I'd barely talked to her since the night she'd given me the cigarettes. Every now and then I'd find another pack left in my bag that I assumed was from her, but I suspected she passed them to me during school hours because we barely had access to each other at home.

She was sneaky about it, though. Most of the time she'd kept a distance. More than once, I'd tried to engage with her in between classes, but even if there was no one else around, she always managed to dodge me or brush me off. It wasn't even like all I wanted to talk about was her father and his abuse—though I definitely wanted to talk about that.

But I also wanted to just...talk. It was weird to live so close to someone who was practically a stranger. To look at her across the dinner table, unable to ask about her day. To work on my homework at my desk and know she was down the hall, her head buried in the same textbook. To stare at the ceiling when I couldn't fall asleep and wonder if she was awake as well.

My curiosity about her felt dangerous, though. For reasons I couldn't express, and so I hadn't made as much effort as I might have. I could have ditched Physics and cornered her in the library before now. Instead of hanging out at the school, I could have walked home with her once or twice. The night of Stark's November educator meeting, I could have tried to approach her instead of inviting Amelia over "to study," turning my radio on full blast, and fucking her with my eyes closed while trying really hard to keep my mind from wandering.

After this afternoon, I'd decided I needed to redefine dangerous.

"We need to talk," I said quietly, plopping in the chair next to her.

She jumped, instinctively trying to hide her magazine. As soon as she realized it was me, she pulled it out again. "No, we don't."

"We do." I pushed the magazine down to see her face. "Stop trying to avoid this. You're the one who warned me about needing to find a way to survive here."

"And it seems you did." Her tone was strangely bitter.

I followed her line of sight, my gaze landing on Amelia.

"Yes. She helps," I admitted. But that wasn't the point of me bringing it up. "How did you know, though?"

"Amelia has loose lips. She's told everyone she's with the new boy. Spoiler if you hadn't figured that out yet."

I fought off the impulse to be irritated about news that Amelia was indeed claiming me as hers. "I meant..." I paused when the librarian walked by until she was out of earshot. "I meant, how did you know I needed a method to survive?"

"I don't know what you're asking."

"You do, but you don't want to say it." I'd thought a lot about this over the last several weeks, especially today during those three hours strapped to Stark's chair, and I was convinced of my theory. "You *know* what your father does to me. At first, I thought you knew because he must have been abusive to everyone. That he punished lots of kids like that. But he doesn't, does he?"

She avoided eye contact. "I guess it depends on your definition of abusive."

"Cut the bullshit, Julianna."

She looked at me then, her jaw tight, her mouth a firm line. "What exactly are you getting at? If you want me to talk straight, maybe you should lead by example."

I thought I'd been pretty forward already, but I zeroed in even more. "Your father doles out severe punishments in that office of his. To me. Did you know that, yes or no?"

She let out a sigh before nodding.

"He doesn't severely punish other kids though, does he?"

Her shoulders sank as she shook her head back and forth.

It was a relief to be validated. Part of me had wondered if everyone was lying, all of us too scared to share our true stories.

But with validation came other emotions. Other questions. "Then how did you know? If he doesn't do this all the time, how did you know he did it to me?"

She shut her magazine, dropped it on the table, and stood up. Without a word, she headed down a row of biographies.

Like hell she was walking away from me. I jumped up after her. "How did you know, Julianna?"

She got to the middle of the row, then turned her head toward me and snapped. "How do you think I knew?"

We were deep in the stacks here, and I realized she'd

led me here, not to avoid the conversation, but to make sure we had more privacy while we had it. "I think you overheard me telling my mother that day," I said, sure of it in hindsight.

"And?"

This was the part that I hated verifying, but it was the answer that made the most sense. "And because he does it to you."

"Ding, ding, ding, ding." She crossed her arms over her chest, like she was trying to guard herself from me, or from saying too much, or because admitting the truth made her feel exposed, which I totally understood.

What I didn't understand was why the hell she ever got punished. "But you never get in trouble."

"And maybe that's why he thinks his punishments work."

I had to think about that longer than I should have.

I was such an idiot.

Of course, that was why she was always so perfectly behaved. Because she knew the repercussions if she wasn't. Just because I'd never seen her get in trouble didn't mean she hadn't in the past.

"How long has he...?" I couldn't finish the question. He was her actual father. She'd lived with him all her life.

"It seems you're figuring that answer out for yourself."

That was hard to get my head around. I'd been dealing with the abuse for a little more than a month and was already at the end of my rope. How had she managed to cope?

Suddenly, I found her promiscuous behavior less curious.

After a silent beat passed, she lowered her defenses. "He's been better since you've been here. Sorry about that. I guess I should say thank you for giving him a distraction."

"You're not welcome."

She let out a defeated breath of air and her shoulders crumpled, and I worried she might cry.

"Don't, don't." I put my hand on her arm to comfort her and felt an unexpected jolt to my pulse that made me drop my hand instantly. "It's really not that bad."

"You don't need to lie."

"Okay, it's pretty shitty."

"I know." She tried to laugh, and it turned into a groan. "I know!"

She covered her face with her hands and shook her head, and for the first time since I'd arrived in Wallingford, I wasn't thinking about myself first.

And it wasn't for me that I said what I said next. "We could tell someone." I'd abandoned that idea after every attempt to talk to my mother had gone badly. With someone else to back me up, it was a different story. I was already trying to decide if it would be better to call the police or tell a teacher. "We could—"

She cut me off with a definitive, "We can't. We can't tell anyone."

"Of course we can. We *have* to tell."

"No one will believe us."

"With both of us—"

She interrupted that notion before I could finish forming it. "Did your mother believe you?"

The mention of my mother stung. I swallowed hard before delivering the excuse I'd formed for her. "She doesn't want to believe anything bad about her husband. She has a stake in the matter. It's not about me."

Julianna's expression softened. She started to reach a hand out to comfort me, but before she made contact, I casually stepped back and leaned a shoulder against the bookshelf, afraid that I'd feel that strange shock again if we touched.

Afraid she'd open up something inside me that I very much wanted to remain closed.

"This community doesn't want to believe anything bad about Langdon Stark," she said, rubbing her fingers against the binding of a random book, as though that had always been what she'd intended to do.

"Then we tell the police."

"It won't make a difference."

"You can't know that."

"I *can* know that. I'm telling you, Cade, all it will do is make things worse." Her subtext was clear—she was speaking from experience.

There was a rustling, and I peeked between the books to see a student taking a novel off the shelf on the other side. After he'd moved on, I asked, "When?"

She knew exactly what I was asking. "A while ago. I was thirteen."

I wanted to know all the details but was well aware of where we were, that we weren't exactly alone, so I focused on what was important. "You're older now. More reliable. Plus, with me—"

"No. No way." She turned and strode to the end of the row, and when she didn't seem surprised that I'd followed, I suspected that once again she hadn't been trying to run away from me.

Even if it wasn't about taking us farther from eaves-droppers, I understood. I felt that same restless burst of energy at times. That same need to run, even though there was nowhere to run to. No one to run to.

"No," she said again when she spun back to me. "I can't. I can't do that. Not again."

Imagining the worst, I tried to reassure her. "What-ever he did, I'm sure it was horrible. But if we get him arrested—"

She cut me off again. "It's not that easy, Cade. People don't want to believe these things about a respected member of the community, and if he finds out we said anything—"

She caught her voice rising and took a beat to calm herself before going on. "It wasn't like you think. It wasn't a big punishment for telling on him. He didn't even guilt trip me, exactly. He...he told me he understood why I was confused. Because I was young and didn't understand that love sometimes was uncomfortable, and that everything he ever did was out of making me a better person, and it was just as hard for him to know I was hurting as it was for him to do the things he had to do, and one day maybe I'd understand how much he truly loves me..."

A tear slipped down her cheek, and before I could think about it, I reached out and wiped it away with my thumb.

I'd been right. That same shock. That same stutter of my heart.

It didn't feel quite as terrifying as it had that first time.

Then because she was staring at me with so much vulnerability, and because she seemed so sad, and because I wanted so much in that moment to be the person who fixed everything for her, and because I'd never had anyone look at me like she did, and because her skin was so soft under my thumb, I trailed it down her cheek and traced her jawline.

"That's not love," I said, softer than anything I'd said so far in our whispered conversation, but with more conviction. Which was saying something, because I didn't have the slightest clue what love was, but I knew it wasn't that. "That's not—"

Another student came around the far end of the aisle, her eyes searching through the rows for a specific book.

My hand fell as Julianna instantly backed away from me, putting distance between us.

I hadn't realized we'd been standing that close until the foot separating us felt too far apart. I hadn't realized how good she smelled or how her bottom lip stuck out when she frowned, how it begged to be...

"It's my senior year, okay?" she whispered, her eyes glancing cautiously toward the student. "I'm so close to getting out of here for good. Six months, and I turn eighteen. Then I'm gone. Please, don't fuck it up by stirring shit now."

At another time, I might have thought it was an unfair request. She wasn't the one in his office every week, and if she'd really suffered at his hand in the past, then she had to know what a terrible thing it was she was asking.

Or I might have realized that I had other options. I could run away. I'd already turned eighteen in October, and even if Stark had the intention of paying for my college, I might have decided that it wasn't worth another six months of abuse.

But right then, all I could think about was the way my thumb was still burning from the touch of Julianna's skin and the trust she tried to hide in her eyes and the way that getting the chance to stand this close to her felt worth any price.

"I'll think about it," I said, storming off before she could stop me or ask any other impossible favor, terrified that next time, the only answer I'd be capable of giving her was yes.

# TEN

## JOLIE

"...AND I'm thankful to have a husband who supports and provides for us like he does. And I'm especially grateful that he's made it possible to spend this holiday with my son, Cade..."

I was only half listening to Carla's gratitude spiel and was busy concentrating on what version of *I'm thankful for my father* I'd give this year. It was the only reason he made us play this game of Go Around the Table and Be Grateful, so he could hear praise heaped on him. For years, it had just been me and him on Thanksgiving, and I was having a hard time getting past what I really wanted to say, which was *I'm grateful to finally not have to bestow all the compliments myself.*

There were other things I was grateful for. Surely.

Careful not to be too obvious about it, I shifted my gaze from Carla to Cade, and my heart stumbled when I found him already looking at me. His expression was stone, but I caught his quick eye roll over his mother's profuse speech and found myself biting back a smile.

"Oh, is it my turn?" he said, quickly looking away from me to my father.

I hadn't even noticed the pause in conversation.

My father's irritation was apparent before he said a word. "It is."

"Sorry about that, sir. I wasn't sure of the order. Let's see..." He was getting better at kissing ass, which was admirable, and hands down it was better for him to stay in line and keep his true self hidden.

But it also made me sad.

I liked his true self. I wanted to know more of it.

"I'm thankful for this food, obviously," he said. "My mom's a great cook."

"And for the person who bought it for us," Carla coached.

He ignored her. "I'm particularly grateful for it this year since I didn't get to have it last year."

I had to pinch my thigh so I wouldn't laugh. He still got those digs in where he could, often to his detriment.

Thankfully, my father hadn't seemed to notice or didn't care since it hadn't been aimed at him.

"Oh, and I'm really grateful for the drama trip tomorrow. It's super cool of Ms. Stacey to arrange an opportunity to spend a night in New York and for our headmaster to approve it." Cade always found a way to avoid addressing my father. He refused to call him Dad, and that was pretty much the only thing my father accepted besides sir.

But that wasn't what had my attention. "Cade's going on the drama trip?"

Dad's eye sparked in that way it always did when he knew he'd upset me. I'd learned a long time ago that he liked me better unhappy, and I often performed that emotion just to stay on his good side.

These days, I rarely let him see any real pain he'd caused, but I'd been too surprised by this hurt to shield it in time.

With a slight smile, my father admonished me. "Wait your turn, Julianna. Cade isn't finished yet."

"Actually, I kind of—"

I stepped on top of his muttering. "Why does Cade get to go on the drama trip?"

The smile faded from my father's lips. "Julianna. You're being rude."

It was a tone I recognized, and usually I was better at heeding the warning. "He said he's done, which means it's my turn, and I'd be grateful to know why Cade gets to go, and I don't."

"This isn't the time to discuss this, Julianna." No, he wanted to discuss it later, when we were alone. When he could punish me immediately for every word that came out of my mouth.

I didn't know exactly what it was that made this battle worth fighting versus every other battle that I ignored, except that it had to do with Cade. Maybe it had been easier to accept that I was treated differently when I was the only child at the school from the Stark household. Or maybe it was because his going was more in my face than the usual extracurricular activities I'd been kept from.

Or maybe it was because I knew Amelia was going too, and thinking of him staying overnight in the city made my stomach turn to stone.

Whatever the reason, I pressed on. "You said it wouldn't be appropriate. Remember? That there was 'too much of an opportunity for corruption,' and that you 'couldn't risk allowing a representative of the Stark name to be put in that environment.' You treat him like he's your son in every other situation. Nothing against you, Cade, but what's different this time?"

"No offense taken," Cade said a bit too cheerfully. I had a feeling he liked someone else being the dissenter for once.

"Is it because he's a guy? Or because you don't care what happens to him in a corrupt environment? Or because you just like seeing me miserable?"

Carla fidgeted at my side. "Julianna..." she cautioned.

"If you must know," my father said over her—he hated when she tried to play peacemaker, preferring to be the one controlling emotions. "Carla signed the permission form without asking me."

"Right. That was me," she said, taking the blame.

Oh.

That's what had been behind her squirming. I saw it now—her downcast eyes. It had been an argument between the two of them, and I felt a little guilty for bringing it up, except that it didn't explain why Cade was still going. Why hadn't my father overridden her permission?

He told me before I'd decided whether or not I was going to ask. "She understands her mistake, and to make up for it, she's agreed to go as one of the chaperones. If Cade gets out of line, the fault will be Carla's."

Wow. I didn't want to be in her position. Even if Cade behaved the entire time, my father would find a way to be angry with his wife. She was set up to fail.

Which, of course, was her punishment. I wondered if she realized that too.

It didn't do any good feeling sorry for her. Her bed had been made, and there was no reason I shouldn't be able to take advantage of it. "If Carla's going, then the problem is solved! She can chaperone me as well as Cade."

Mostly Cade, though. She could keep him from sneaking out of his room to be with Amelia.

"No," my father said. As expected. "I'm not going to put that much on Carla."

"I really don't mind—" she began.

"It's too much responsibility for you." Coming from someone else, it might have sounded like he was only looking out for his wife. From my father, it was clear to everyone that he didn't believe she could handle it. That he wouldn't even give her the opportunity to prove she could.

I wasn't especially fond of my stepmother, but we did share an unspoken camaraderie. The only two women in a traditional household—it was impossible not to be somewhat bonded. "She could handle it," I said, breaking one of the most important of my father's rules— no ganging up on him. "I wouldn't give her any trouble at all."

"I said no."

It was past the point of when I should have dropped it.

Still, I tried another of his favorite tactics: flattery. "You know what, Daddy? You should come too! Make it a family trip. You're so committed to your work and to us. When do you get a break? You deserve a—"

"I said no!" The table shook from the force of his fist against it. "Cade and Carla will leave as planned in the morning, and while they are gone, it seems you and I will need to have a lengthy discussion about your behavior today."

My stomach sank, taking my whole body with it. It had been a while since I'd had to suffer through "a lengthy discussion." I'd gotten so incredibly good at following the rules, and having Carla and Cade around had given my father other targets. With the two of us alone, it would be especially bad.

My fault. I'd known better. I shouldn't have pushed.

I couldn't swallow past the ball in my throat to offer an apology, though, and I knew he was waiting for one.

He only gave it a few seconds before lashing out again. "You've ruined Thanksgiving, Julianna. I don't even want to hear what you're grateful for now, and the food is getting cold. Pass the yams, Carla. Hopefully, the cooking will salvage the meal."

I tried to be thankful that I'd at least gotten out of the torture of that speech, but I knew it was another mark against me. Another thing I'd be "talked to" about this weekend. It was hard not to agree with him—I had ruined Thanksgiving. Not that the day was all that special to begin with. There wasn't any day in this house that was special. There were just days that were easier to survive than others.

Today was looking like an "other."

Heavy silence shrouded us for the rest of dinner. The cooking, it turned out, was not good enough to salvage anything. Not for me, anyway. Everything tasted the same, none of it very good, and soon I was moving things around on my plate more than I was putting them in my mouth. In the quiet, the rhythmic tick-tock of the grandfather clock sounded loud, boring into my head until I couldn't help but think it wasn't the clock at all, but the ticking of a bomb hidden deep inside me, getting closer and closer to going off.

The second my father put down his fork, I jumped up. "I'll start cleanup."

I gathered my dishes and Carla's—she was busy loading my father up with a second plate, which thankfully I wasn't required to sit through—and headed into the kitchen, but not before Cade jumped up as well. "I'm done too."

"You aren't going to eat more?" Carla sounded as hurt about this as if he'd turned down a hug. "It's Thanksgiving!"

"Saving room for pie," he said, then the door shut

behind me, and I didn't hear anything else until he was pushing into the kitchen with his own dishes. "Thank God that meal is over. How about adding that to my gratitude list?"

I feigned a laugh, still too upset to give him anything sincere, and started in on the dishwasher. It was my nightly chore to load. Cade's chore was to help his mother clean up the table and then take out trash, and later he'd put the dishes away. Before he'd arrived, I'd been in charge of all of it and was generally happy with how the jobs had been divvied up, even if I found it a bit sexist.

Except it was a holiday.

Which meant we'd used a lot of cooking dishes plus the china. And that meant handwashing the china since it wasn't dishwasher safe, as well as the dishes that didn't fit in the first load since my father refused to let anything sit in the sink for more than the space of a meal.

So I was still elbows deep in suds by the time the dining room table was cleared and Cade had returned from his trip outside with the garbage.

I didn't turn to look behind me when he came back in, but the hair stood up at the back of my neck, and I could swear he was staring at me.

"Want some help?" he said after a minute.

Teeth gritted, I shook my head, quite used to being alone in my misery.

"Let me rephrase—because I'm pretty sure you don't know how to accept a favor—move over, and hand me a dish." He was reaching for the rose-patterned china plate in my hand before I'd even noticed he was next to me, sleeves rolled up, ready to rinse.

I scowled, unpracticed at receiving anything good—he was right about me there—but I handed him the plate all the same, and with him by my side, I wondered if I'd been too hasty the week before in the library when I'd told him we couldn't do anything about my father.

I hadn't changed my mind about the inability to get away with it. But I was mad, and anger made the revenge fantasy so much sweeter.

I didn't get even a full minute of daydreaming in before Cade interrupted it. "I'm sorry." When I didn't say anything, he added, "For the trip. I hadn't realized he was the reason you hadn't signed up."

I gave him an incredulous stare. "You can't be that naive."

He laughed. "I can be. Mostly because I didn't think too much about it. And I didn't think too much about it because I didn't want to feel guilty about it. I'm sorry for that too."

It helped, and it didn't. I wasn't ready to let go of my wrath, but it wasn't him I was mad at. "I'm the one who should be apologizing to you." I handed him another plate. "He could have said you couldn't go anymore just because I brought it up."

Of course, then he wouldn't have the opportunity to administer a lengthy punishment. Not that having Carla or Cade around made much difference. When my father shut himself in a room with someone, everyone else knew better than to interrupt.

"Wouldn't have been the end of the world," he said with a shrug.

Again, the look I gave him said I didn't believe him for one second.

He grinned. "All right. It would have sucked ass, but I get it. I didn't take it personally at all."

I hadn't really been feeling guilty about it, but I did appreciate the permission not to.

"And you didn't ruin Thanksgiving," he continued. "It was terrible to begin with."

"It was terrible to begin with," I said at the exact same time.

We laughed, and I handed him another plate. "I'm not usually so bothered by how terrible it is," I said when the amusement had faded. "I don't look at it, really. But it all stacks up, and it's like there must be a sensor in my brain that doesn't register until the terribleness gets to a certain point, and then an alarm goes off, and I have to look, and when I do the only way I can react is to just...grrrr." My grip tightened on the dish in my hand as I pretended I was shaking my father.

"I honestly don't know how you do it. I think I would have gone crazy by now."

"Who says I haven't?"

"Even the way he talks to you is infuriating. 'Julianna, you're being rude.'" He mocked my father with an accuracy that made me have to attempt the same.

"'Julianna, don't interrupt.'" I scrubbed at the cranberry stain. "'Julianna, be perfect.' I don't know if it's the way he says it or the name in general, but I hate it. I hate what it stands for. I hate who she is. Julianna Who Does Everything Right. Julianna Who Never Upsets Him. She's so proper. So well behaved. What if that's not who I really am? What if I'm really someone else? Someone not Julianna."

"Julie," he suggested.

I cringed. "Too close."

"Jerico."

"Too far off." I sighed. "That's the problem. I've been so trained to be Julianna, I'd never look up if anyone called me something else."

I thought that had ended it, but then he said, "Jolie," and something happened in my chest. A pinching of some kind, like grabby hands clutching onto a much-wanted gift, refusing to let it go.

"Yeah, that's who I am. Jolie." Whether I liked it because it fit me or because he'd chosen it, I didn't know, but I instantly claimed it.

He tilted his head to study me. "Yeah? What are you like, Jolie?"

"Well, I'm not quiet, that's for sure." I passed the plate on, jolting at the zing through my body when I accidentally brushed his hand in the process. Hoping he didn't see my reaction, I turned away to grab another from the stack. "I'm very loud. And I openly smoke. And I kiss whatever boy I want when I want to. And I say 'fuck you' at the dinner table. And when I'm mad, I show I'm mad."

"Yeah, you do," he said, encouraging me. "How do you show you're mad?"

I let out an excited sort of giggle. Permission to express myself was not something anyone ever gave me, including myself, and it was empowering to imagine what I could do with that.

It was even more exciting that it was him who had given the permission. "I'd fucking tear out all the plants in that stupid garden of his, for one."

"Odd place to start, but I'll join you for it."

"And I'd take a sledgehammer to that lock he keeps on my door. And I'd take scissors to all his ties. And those short uniform skirts he makes us wear. And I'd break all his favorite albums in half. And his record player. I'd break everything I could get my hands on that he cared about. *Everything.* Every. Single. Thing."

The anger was too real, and giving voice to the things I fantasized made it too easy to get caught up in the destruction that I so very badly wanted to wield, and so when the impulse to throw the plate I was holding to the floor popped up, I didn't have time to calm myself down before I was hurling the dish across the room.

It hit the ground with a satisfying shatter.

Yes. That was exactly who I wanted to be.

We stared at the pieces of china for several seconds, my heart thudding like I'd just run the PE loop around the garden in record time.

"Oh, yeah," Cade said, and when his eyes hit mine, they locked onto some deep part of me, and suddenly, it felt like we were connected. Like the most basic parts of me were controlled by him. Like I didn't even breathe on my own anymore, and I didn't *want* to. I just wanted to keep being breathed by him.

Then reality hit. "Oh, shit."

I reached for a towel to dry off then went for the broom and dustpan. Cade was already stooped over the mess when I got back, several large pieces in his hands. "Probably too broken to just glue together."

He was joking. It was *definitely* too broken.

"He's going to kill me," I said, feeling that all-too-familiar panic. It was bad enough knowing I'd angered my father when I didn't deserve it. There was nothing I could do to prevent that wrath. When I brought it on myself, I only had one person to blame. "This was my grandma's china. I'm not going to be able to walk for days."

Cade's expression was hard to read, but his eyes looked...concerned? "Maybe he won't notice. We'll clean it up; I'll take the pieces to the trash. He won't notice until Christmas when there's a plate missing." He knew that meant we'd just be delaying an inevitable punishment, so he added, "We'll deal with it then."

*I'd* deal with it. Not *we*.

Because he hadn't been the one to throw the plate. It hadn't even been his chore to deal with the dishes in the first place.

But before I could correct him, the door opened, and there was my father. "What was that crashing sound?" His eyes landed on us, giving him his answer. "What the hell did you do, Cade?"

The *wrong* answer, it turned out. Since Cade was

the one holding the pieces, it was easy to see where he'd gotten the impression.

"No, no. It was me," I said quickly. "My hands were wet, and it just slipped out of my grip." That didn't explain how the dish had gotten all the way over here by the wall, and my father wasn't stupid.

He'd add it to my previous transgressions. He'd be sure I suffered for it.

"Don't do that for me," Cade said, standing up in a rush. I gave him a puzzled look, but he'd turned his attention to my father. "She's trying to cover for me, sir. I was horsing around and dropped it."

My father adopted his Very Mad face, which looked a lot like a Very Happy face in some respects. "This was my mother's china," he said. "It's an heirloom. They don't make replacements."

"I understand, sir, and I'm sorry."

"To my office. Now." He didn't have to say he expected me to finish cleaning the mess up. "And you can forget about that drama trip of yours. Expect to spend this weekend with me."

I could have spoken up, and I should have. But Cade shook his head sharply when I tried, and I knew enough about my father to guess that, if I tried to take the blame now, he'd rather punish us both than exert the effort to get to the real truth.

But I thought about it. The words were still at the tip of my tongue when Cade headed off to where he'd been sent. Were on the brink of falling out when my father paused to kiss my forehead.

By the time he'd left, following after Cade, they'd dissolved into nothing.

I brought the back of my hand to my mouth, holding back a sob. Guilt shook my body, but that wasn't the most overwhelming emotion.

Finally, for the first time that day, I was grateful.

Grateful that he hadn't let me tell the truth. Grateful that he'd helped me with the dishes in the first place. Grateful that he wasn't going on that trip with Amelia. Grateful that he'd found a way into my otherwise terrible life. Grateful that he'd let my father abuse him this time instead of me.

So grateful that it didn't occur to me until later to wonder why.

# ELEVEN
## CADE

GRABBING both my sweater and my undershirt together as I pushed through the door, I had them half off when I noticed my room wasn't empty.

"Jesus, Julianna." It only took a second to recover from surprise and move on to panic. "What the hell are you doing? You can't be in here."

Nothing had ever been said about being in each other's bedrooms, but I didn't need to be given a rule to know her father wouldn't like it. He confined her to her own room most of the time and had a deadbolt on the outside of her door. It was pretty obvious he wouldn't want her down the hall in mine.

I might not have been so concerned about pushing my limits if I wasn't already coming directly from a punishment—a punishment that hadn't even been mine.

I still didn't know why I'd taken the fall for her.

Or if I did know, I wasn't interested in admitting it.

"I needed to talk to you," she said in a whispered tone, as if her father could hear what we said from the floor below us. I was pretty positive he couldn't really hear us, but I completely understood the desire to be cautious.

It was the same desire that had me desperate to get her off my bed and out the door. "This is really not a good time. You need to leave."

She stood up, which was a relief, but also a distraction, especially when she didn't make any other move to go. While I'd been in her father's office, taking the blame for the broken dish, she'd gotten ready for bed. Two months I'd been in her house, and this was the first time I'd seen her in anything besides her school uniform and father-approved casual clothing. Tonight, she was in a nightie.

And it was short.

And pretty damn see-through.

Fuck. I was going to hell for staring at her tits like I was. For wanting to touch them. For wanting to rub my thumbs over the taut peaks.

Of course, I was already *in* hell, so it probably didn't matter what shitty thing I did, except that it would be pretty goddamn embarrassing to get a boner in front of my stepsister.

I ran my free hand over my face. I'd skipped my shave since it was a holiday, and the feel of stubble on my palm gave me something to concentrate on so that the blood wouldn't run south. My other hand was at my neck, still clutching the clothing that I'd only managed to get half off, and after a few seconds, I realized that maybe that was a good thing because she was too busy looking at my bare chest to notice how I'd been staring at hers.

I knew it was stupid to make anything of that.

I had a normal, average teenage male body, nothing impressive. Whether she'd seen many men shirtless or not, I had no idea. Her reputation didn't shed any light on the matter. Shirts didn't have to come off to do the kinds of things she was known to do. So she was probably looking because bare skin was new to her. Or she was curious. Definitely not because she found me attractive.

Still, her eyes on me made me stand a little taller. And when she lifted her gaze and saw that I'd seen where she'd been looking, her cheeks flushed. "I'll be quick, I just need to know—oh, God. What did he do to you?"

I'd heard something—movement downstairs, and not a threat at all—but I'd made the mistake of turning back toward the door when I heard it, and that gave her a view of my back.

Somehow letting her see that was more embarrassing than an erection. "It's nothing; will you go?"

I started to put my shirt back on, but she was already at my side, already turning me so she could look at my lower back. "Just...let me see."

Her hand on my bare skin burned, almost the way the marks on my back had burned, and also not like it at all. Her burn hurt because it was dangerous. Because it was forbidden. Because I didn't want only her hand touching me but her whole body.

It pulled my focus long enough for her to get a look at the thing I didn't want her to see, especially when I'd yet to see it for myself, and when her breath hitched, I knew it was as bad as I'd feared.

"What?" I craned my head over my shoulder, impossibly trying to see the small of my back. "What is it?"

She brought her hand to her mouth, her eyes watering as she shook her head.

A flash of frustrated energy surged through me. I threw open the door and stormed down the hall to the bathroom. I didn't have a mirror in my room, and since I wasn't lucky enough to have an en suite like she did, I had to use the one down the hall.

Though, maybe I was the lucky one, because otherwise, I might have had a lock on my door too.

I shut the door behind me and took my sweater off the rest of the way, dropping it to the floor before turning my head to look in the mirror to examine what Stark had left on my skin. They were low on my back—he'd made me hold my shirt up while he'd done it. Not so deep that they'd scar, but deep enough that they were bleeding. Three words. Scratched into my skin with a piece of the broken china because he seemed to enjoy making the punishment fit the crime whenever possible.

*I AM NOTHING*

As sadistic as it was, it hadn't hurt as much as some of his other methods of discipline. It had been a constant pain, which was somehow easier to bear and prepare for than the surprise sting of a whip. I'd bit down on the back of my hand, which now had a pretty severe hickey, and had tried to guess the design of his strokes but had gotten lost with all the ups and downs of the M and the N and had no longer been sure he'd been writing words at all.

But of course he had.

Words that would hurt long after the physical pain subsided.

"It's not true, okay? It's not true."

I turned my head from the awful image to see Julianna had followed me into the bathroom. I should have locked the fucking door.

But it was already too late.

She'd already seen the words in my bedroom. She already knew.

My eye twitched, and I couldn't look at her. "Go away, Julianna."

"I liked it when you called me Jolie," she said, her back pressed to the closed door, as far as she could be from me and still be in the same room.

*Yeah, right, it wasn't true.*

"Go away, Jolie," I said, louder than I should have. I didn't care for the moment what happened to me if we were caught alone together, even though I really should care. Even though I would care about what would happen to her if I gave myself a second to think about it.

She took a timid step toward me, and despite feeling humiliated and raw, I caught myself stealing another glance at her breasts, and lower, the outline of her white cotton panties, and felt the blood rush to my cock.

"You can't let him get inside your head," she said.

*Fuck.*

He was already in there. And she was too. Two people who couldn't be more different. One pulling me into darkness. The other one...

The other one didn't belong.

"Go. The Fuck. Away." My jaw was clenched so tightly, the words came out focused and sharp and mean, and if there had been something satisfying to throw in that bathroom, I would have been hurling it at the door behind her, damn the consequences. I needed to be able to sit with this; alone. Needed to sneak out on the roof and smoke my cigarettes in the freezing cold.

She hesitated, the act of deciding written on her face. "I, uh—"

"Go!"

"But I need to know something first!" she said rapidly. Without giving me a chance to reply, she went on. "I need to know why."

My brows drew inward, and for a confused second I thought she was asking why her father had chosen to carve those particular words on me, then realized she was asking why I'd taken the blame.

Ironically, they were both sort of the same answer, but I really didn't want to get into that with her. "You've helped me too," I said, hoping a reply would get her out of there. "The cigarettes. The mints."

"It's not the same."

"How is it not the same?"

"That was camaraderie. This was... This was a sacrifice. I didn't risk myself for you. I didn't put myself on the line." She sounded angry.

Which struck me as ironic. Here I was with every reason to be angry at her—for breaking the plate, for making me want to act noble. For being soft and kind and out of place in a house that was only hard and cruel and punishing.

I let out a laugh as I reached for the towel to wipe off the blood on my back. I'd get in trouble for staining the tan fabric, but I was experienced enough now to know that toilet paper and tissue made the wound hurt worse when it stuck to the skin. "I didn't have an ulterior motive, if that's what you're asking. Don't worry about it, okay? Go."

"But why!"

Her tone was drenched in desperation, the kind of desperation that had a weight, and when it got its claws in you, and you pushed it away, it invariably took something from you at the same time.

From me, her desperation pulled the truth. "Because it *is* true. These words on my back? Your father carved them because he sees what I am. I *am* nothing, and I'll always be nothing, and it doesn't matter what happens to nothing the way it matters what happens to—"

I stopped myself. Partly because whatever came next would have been too much. Mostly because I hadn't quite formulated in my mind what it was that she was. But it wasn't nothing. It was very, very much not nothing.

She'd moved closer during my rant. Too close. And

when she opened her mouth, I was sure she was about to deliver some consoling platitude or insist that I was wrong when it was so very obvious that I wasn't.

But instead, she stood on her tiptoes and leaned forward, and I was so stunned that her mouth was already brushing against mine when I had the sense to step back. "What the fuck are you doing?"

Her heels came back to the ground, but she didn't move. She kept staring at me, barely blinking, and I noticed for the first time that there were green flecks in her blue eyes, and that she had a sweet scent I couldn't place, and that I wished that I was dumb enough to lean in instead of away.

No.

This was trouble. *She* was trouble. Being anywhere near her would get us both in *too much* trouble.

"You can't fucking do this," I said, feeling like something more needed to be said. For me as much as her.

Then I dropped the towel and picked up my sweater. Trying my best not to let any part of my body touch her, I moved past her, out of the bathroom, to my room, and told myself I wasn't disappointed when she didn't follow.

# TWELVE

## CADE

I MANAGED to avoid Julianna for a total of nine days.

Even when the trip was canceled, Stark made my mother still go—her punishment for signing me up in the first place—which meant the entire weekend was spent at his whim. Thankfully, he was on a kick about tidying up the school grounds, so I endured hours in the cold, cutting back dead hedges and picking up litter.

It was better than enduring time in his office.

I told myself it was better than being anywhere near Julianna, too.

Her punishment for speaking back at dinner was dealt with indoors, and as much as I wanted to know what it was, I knew it was best to pretend I didn't care.

When Monday came around, we were back to the school routine, and that was easier. Our class schedule dictated our separation. At night, we were in our rooms doing homework, like always. At dinner, I learned how to keep my eyes on my plate. I didn't offer to help her with dishes. I didn't even come in the kitchen to unload the dishwasher until well after I knew she'd be gone.

It was dumb. I knew that. Dumb to worry about being in the same room with her or what might happen if our eyes met. Both had happened plenty of times in the past, and her father had never cared. She'd never tried to kiss me. It wasn't like I expected she'd try again.

The problem was that I hoped she'd try again.

And if she didn't, there was a good chance I'd try to kiss her, and just thinking about kissing her got me all tangled up because then I wanted to think about what would happen next. And then next after that. But instead of staying focused on the next that would invariably lead to being murdered by my stepfather, I would get stuck on the next that had her in my arms. In my bed.

Under my body.

So I didn't only avoid her. I avoided thinking about her.

Easy enough until the following Saturday, Stark decided it was time to get the house decorated for the holidays. All for show, of course. Not for the enjoyment of the people who lived inside, but for what a Christmas tree in the window said to people outside.

"You can put up the lights on the house after you bring in the boxes of ornaments from storage," he said to me. "Julianna will take care of the tree."

He'd had that delivered, though he had threatened to

drop me off in the woods and make me bring one back myself. He found my horror satisfying enough to not have to actually follow through, but I hadn't been entirely sure he wasn't sincere until the delivery man had shown up early that morning with a fresh-cut pine.

"And I'll fill the house with the scent of gingerbread," my mother said, cheerily keeping up her image as the dutiful homemaker.

Stark turned an accusing glare on her. "You've already forgotten I detest the spice? What do you use that brain for, Carla? Sometimes I think we need to enroll you in the academy, except that we have an IQ requirement, and I doubt you'd qualify."

Flustered, she somehow kept a smile on her face. "I meant poppyseed bread. I don't know why I said gingerbread. Vanilla is the spice you love. I didn't forget."

As much as I resented my mother these days, it enraged me to hear her referred to as stupid. Not that I was about to defend her—I wasn't stupid either.

Instead, I drew the attention back to me. "I haven't ever been in the storage shed. Will the boxes be easy to find?"

Asking questions was always a risk of its own. Stark hated explaining himself. On the other hand, he hated it when things were done wrong.

He narrowed his eyes at me, and I held my breath, waiting for the lashing.

What he said was worse. "Julianna? Go with and show him."

If she looked at me at all before saying, "Yes, sir," I didn't see it because I definitely did not look at her.

"Good. Dress warm. I wouldn't want you to already be frozen before you have to get on the roof."

Somehow I doubted his sincerity.

I took his advice, anyway, dressing in layers because it was a good way to stall, not because I was fearful of the cold, but eventually I couldn't put it off any longer, and the two of us set out to the rickety storage shed in the backyard.

"This is chaos," I said when I flicked on the light and saw the disaster ahead of us. Closest to the door was all the garden equipment—the mower and a wheelbarrow and hoses and shovels and rakes. There was also a generator along one wall. Beyond that were the totes. Dozens and dozens of them. None of them labeled or organized. Many, I suspected, hadn't been opened in years. "They have to be near the front, right? Since you used them last year?"

"Maybe." She didn't sound hopeful. "He had the generator set up last spring. Before that, a bunch of the totes were in its place. They've all been moved around now."

"Well, shit."

"Yeah."

She closed the door, and I tensed, wary about being in a confined space with her with the door shut, but as soon as I realized that it was warmer without the wind blowing in, I decided I was going to have to suck it up.

Though, the cold might have been easier to endure.

"Better get started." Faster we were out of here, the better.

It only took five minutes before I realized that this wasn't going to be a quick chore. Not with Julianna. A quick peek under the lid of each tote told me what was inside, and I was able to eliminate a whole tower of them right away. She, on the other hand, found a lot to distract her.

"My angel costume!" she said after opening one. She pulled out a headband with a halo and put it on her head, then rummaged around a bit before retrieving a crumpled set of wings. "This was my Halloween costume for third grade."

She stuck her arms through the elastics and turned around to shake the flimsy things in my direction.

Damn, she was adorable.

"Your father let you go trick-or-treating?" I couldn't imagine it. That was the only reason I wanted to know.

"Of course not. There was a parade at school, and he couldn't let me be the only one without a costume." She feigned a gasp. "What would people think?"

She took off the wings and tried to straighten out the bent wire. "He chose the angel. I wanted to be a witch."

Now that sounded like him. "I'm surprised he let you go to school at all before you got to middle school and he could police you all the time as the headmaster." Stark Academy started enrollment at sixth grade. I'd never wondered where she'd gone before that.

"It was almost worse that he did. I don't know if I would have realized that my family wasn't normal." She put the wings back in the tote and rooted around a bit more before returning the lid and moving it to the ground so she could look in the one underneath it.

It continued from there—every lid lifted revealing another memory.

I knew I should rush her along. But for some reason, I let her take the trip to the past while I worked, listening to her prattle on about this item or that, wishing I didn't like hearing her talk so much.

Most of it wasn't even happy talk. Every object held the same sorts of addendums—*This was how my father stained this memory. This is how he stained that one.* Every recollection another record of proof that Langdon Stark was a monster.

I'd gotten through almost half of the totes with no success when I realized she'd been quiet for a whole minute. I dared a glance at her and found her staring intently at a photograph.

I didn't want to be interested.

I really, really didn't want to be.

But there I was, setting down my tote so I could go and look over her shoulder. There was a woman in the image, with light eyes and long blonde/brown hair, the same shade as Julianna's.

It wasn't hard to guess who it was. "Your mother?"

"Yeah."

I bit my cheek and held my tongue. For all of ten seconds. "Do you remember her?"

"A little. I was only four when she died. But I remember

that she hummed a lot, which irritated my father to no end. And she liked cats. She used to feed this black and white stray." She thought a minute, remembering that silly halo bobbing above her head. "I was so young...of course, I didn't really understand what death was, but when Dad said she wasn't coming back, that was what I was worried most about—that cat. Who was going to feed the damn cat?"

"What happened to it?" I whispered the question, sure I knew the answer, wishing I could ignore the need to have it confirmed.

"I fed him for a while. I'd run out every day as soon as I woke up and take a handful from the bag, just the way my mother did. But then the bag was empty. So I told Dad." She took a deep breath. "It didn't go well."

She smiled in that way that said what she was thinking about was terrible, but if she didn't show it, maybe it wouldn't hurt so much. "I think that was when I really knew, you know. Because he's always been like he is. That didn't just start after she was gone. He was always awful, and she was as helpless to it as we all are, but when she was here, I always knew there was a lap waiting for me after. So that time with the cat—that was when I really got that I was alone."

I'd never been particularly empathetic, and maybe I wasn't then either, but it was the only word I had to explain the intensity of the need I had to want to console her. Console both the Julianna from the past and the one standing in front of me, though the one standing in front of me didn't necessarily look in need of consolation. She was strong. Stronger than me, in many ways. In most ways.

And the methods I would have used to console the Julianna from the past versus the one in front of me—well, those were very different. G-rated methods versus R. X, even, if I let myself think about it too long, which I knew better than to do.

"I'm sorry about the cat," I said, deciding it was the safest way around this conversation.

"Oh, the cat was fine. Janice ended up adopting him."

"Janice the gardener?" I'd worked with her a few times over the past months, usually as part of detention that I was sure I never deserved.

"Yeah. I don't know how she found out about the cat. Maybe I told her, or maybe he was never really a stray and was hers all along, I don't know. But she'd babysit me from time to time, usually at our house, but once I went to hers, and there he was."

I let out a sound that was almost like a laugh. "Who'd have thought there could be a happy ending in this place?"

"Right?" She cleared her throat, dropping the picture back in the tote before putting the lid back on it. "Anyway, the impression I have of my mother is that she was a lot like Carla."

I'd moved back to the tote I'd abandoned already but paused before I lifted the lid. "Subservient and neglectful?"

She gave a wry smile as she pushed the lid in my

hand up farther to peek inside. "I meant traditional—a good cook and homemaker. A woman who made her husband feel important. But I could see how you'd label them both with less flattering adjectives. This isn't Christmas. Next."

I put the tote to the side and reached for the next one, puzzling over her choice of descriptors. She might be able to understand my labels, but I couldn't understand hers.

"You really only think those things about your mom?" As though she could see the inside of my head.

"Yes. Yes. Definitely yes." This tote had videotapes with handwritten descriptions like *La Bohème* and *La Traviata*. "Well, maybe that's not true. I should add manipulative and self-serving. She's real good at wooing men. Her problem is getting them to stick around.

"Move over so I can grab that one, will you?" I scooted her with my hip, regretting it as soon as our bodies met. Even through my coat and three layers of shirts, I felt the zing from the contact.

Either she didn't notice or she didn't mind because she moved, but not so much that we weren't still touching. "You really don't have any good memories with her?"

Fuck, were we still talking about my mom?

I considered not answering. This tote had ornaments in it. The rest of the ones we needed were probably underneath, which meant we were done and could get out of here.

But she was good at pulling things from me. Like a fishing line, except her hook didn't have any bait, and I didn't know why I kept swallowing it unless maybe I secretly liked the tortured feeling of saying too much to her, of being too exposed. Of splitting myself open and letting her see what was inside.

"She used to read to me," I said. "Picture books. Every one she could get her hands on. She was never really a library kind of gal, and we rarely had money for things, so she'd go to garage sales or take hand-me-downs. Dr. Seuss and The Wild Things one and Berenstein Bears."

"Beren*stain* Bears," she corrected with a grin.

"Whatever the fuck it was. I had *Inside, Outside, Upside Down* memorized. She'd use funny voices to keep me interested—or to keep herself interested—and run her hands through my hair. Kiss me on my head."

I barely recognized that woman in Carla.

I didn't recognize myself as that little boy at all. It didn't even feel like it had happened to me, but rather like a movie I once saw. "I think once I started to think for myself, she didn't know what to do with me. Maybe it got harder. Maybe *I* got harder. I don't know. Just... I learned to read for myself, and she stopped sitting with me, and she stopped getting me new books, and soon she stopped thinking about me much at all."

"We both lost our mothers young," she said. "Only you never knew, so you didn't get to grieve."

Yeah, that was it. That was...on the nose and so well said and no one had ever made me feel like they got it until right then.

Which made my chest constrict.

And my throat feel tight.

And the layers of clothing must have done the trick because I was suddenly hot and sweating. And she was standing so close, and I could feel her breath on my chin like the world's tiniest space heater. And all I wanted to do was capture that breath inside me, take it all in. Make it mine.

"You aren't alone anymore, Jolie." Goddamn hook. Tugging out words I shouldn't say. Calling her a name that was too intimate. Pulling my mouth down as hers moved up.

Something inside me was still thinking right because when her lips grazed mine, I said, "Don't." Which was the thing to say, and the thing to do.

But I didn't push her away, and she moved her mouth over mine again, softly. Teasing? Testing, before she closed her lips around mine.

I jumped back instantly. Fast, as though there'd been electricity in her kiss. "Don't," I said again.

Only one breath passed—a simple rise and fall of her chest—and then I was lunging forward, pushing her up against the tower of totes, my hands clenched around her upper arms while I kissed the fuck out of her.

Devoured her.

Like I'd never get a chance again, and there was a real good reason to think that was the case. Open-mouthed and punishing. Taking more than I was giving. Sliding my tongue in too far. Tasting her. Memorizing her. Kissing an angel.

She groaned, and I took that too, swallowing it as I

pressed harder into her, grinding the ache in my jeans against her belly. I could feel her struggling, and I knew if I let her arms go, she'd touch me. Anywhere she touched me, any way she touched me, it would be heaven.

But I wanted her captive.

*Needed* her captive. Needed to feel like this was my decision instead of like I had no choice but to touch her. She made me too out of control, otherwise. Made me feel like I was a black hole, and whether I wanted to or not, I would draw all of her inside of me.

I would break her then.

Maybe not by my own hand, but she would be broken apart if she really got in. She'd be shattered, and her father would kill us both, and fuck. Fuck. I wouldn't care. For this one single moment, I wouldn't even care.

Abruptly, light spilled in the shed, and thank God for the yard equipment and that we were all the way in the back because even though we jumped apart instantly, we would have been caught otherwise.

"What's taking you two so long?" Stark said.

For the first time since I'd met her, I saw real fear in Jolie's eyes, a fear that somehow looked more severe with the halo on. I'd wondered before if her punishments were as severe as mine, if she really had a sense of how far her father could go. It wasn't the kind of thing I could ask, and she managed to piss him off so much less than I did, it was an obvious assumption.

Now, though, I was sure that she knew. She knew

just how evil he was. She knew just how much she should be afraid.

Her fear sprung me into action. "It took us a while to find the Christmas stuff, sir, but these should be them." I lifted the last tote I'd looked in as evidence. "I should label them this year after the holiday before I put them back."

I did everything right. Called him sir. Assumed responsibility for making the task easier in the future. Let him know I was aware that I'd be the one storing them again.

I'd been learning from his daughter, after all.

"Smart thinking, Cade. Who knew you had it in you." He scanned his daughter then me, looking both of us up and down, his eyes lingering on her halo, and I silently prayed that he assumed her flushed cheeks and red lips were from the cold.

It felt like forever before he spoke again. "Make sure you clean off any mouse droppings before you bring those things inside. If any of us get Hantavirus, it will be your fault." He looked back at Jolie. "Probably shouldn't be handling anything in those totes, Julianna, but if you're determined, let him clean it off first. Better if he got sick than you."

I hated him. I legitimately hated him.

And even though he seemed to think better of her than he did of me, I hated him most because of whatever things he'd done to her. Because of that fear he'd programmed into her eyes.

She didn't seem to breathe again until he was gone. "I swear I almost had a heart attack."

My heart was racing too. For entirely different reasons than they'd been racing before. I set down the tote, and when I lifted my hands, they were shaking. "That was stupid. We were stupid."

"I know," she agreed, removing the halo and tossing it to the ground. "We have to be more careful."

My eyes flew to hers. *Be more careful?* No. That fucking couldn't happen again. No fucking way.

But it was hard to say when she was looking at me like that, like I was the only light in her world, and though it was possible I was just dark in disguise, I understood how much she needed to believe otherwise.

And I really did want her.

Wanted her to be my light, too.

She took a step forward, putting her hand on my cheek. "Cade..."

I shook my head, looking for strength I wasn't sure I had. If she couldn't protect herself, it had to be me.

"Stop. Don't do that. Don't say we can't have this. Don't say *I* can't have this."

Her pleading wore me down. It also hardened my resolve. "This is for *you*," I said, taking her hand from my face. I grabbed the other one with it, held them together. "It's not for me." I was pretty sure I'd suffer anything from her father's hand, if that was the only price to be paid.

But it wasn't.

"This can't happen again."

It was her turn to shake her head.

"It can't," I repeated. Bending in, I kissed her quickly, once more because I couldn't bear not to.

Then I picked up the tote and left, putting distance between us, determined that I would be the one to keep her safe.

I HATE HER.

The inside cover of my notebook was filled with that refrain, over and over. *I hate her, I hate her, I hate her, I hate her.*

I hated her pretty little laugh.

I hated her jet-black hair.

I hated her adoring smile.

I hated how nice she was.

Most of all, I hated that she had the one thing I wanted most: Cade.

The biggest problem with hating Amelia Lu was how much I actually didn't hate her. She'd been at Stark since sixth grade. We'd come into the academy together, and she was by all counts the sweetest girl in the whole school. We'd never been friends, per se—there was no being friends with the headmaster's daughter—but she'd been the closest thing to it. She'd never backed away when I entered a room or whispered behind my back as soon as I walked by. When her grandmother died the year before, she'd let me hug her when I gave her condolences, and she'd squeezed so hard, I'd been the one who had to pull away.

So it was a real shame to have such venomous feelings toward her now. Real, real shame.

I finished coloring in the block letters of the latest version of the phrase I'd drawn, this time on the borders of the Winter Talent Exhibition program, then stole a glance down the row to where she was seated.

Big mistake.

Because she wasn't just holding Cade's hand and giggling like she had been the last time I'd peeked. Now they were making out like they were at the local movie theater instead of in the school auditorium.

**I REALLY FUCKING HATE HER.**

I drew the words so aggressively that the program tore. It hadn't been high-quality paper, to be fair. My father boasted a quality school, but he was cheap when he had the opportunity.

The annual Winter Talent Exhibition, for example. Everyone knew it was a bullshit day. Half of the school had already gone home for the break. The rest of us had to endure ninety minutes of poetry recitations, piano performances, and choir renditions of holiday songs. With so many empty chairs in the three-hundred-fifty-seat auditorium, there was plenty of space for students to stretch out or break off in cliques.

Or, in Cade and Amelia's case, in couples.

And since my father had already left with an unruly bunch of tenth graders, the couples were now free to get coupling.

Another glance from me down the row—I couldn't help myself—this time my gaze smacked right into Cade's. He was still kissing Amelia, but his eyes were open, watching me, and as if to prove this whole relationship with her was only about pushing me away, he waited until he was sure I was looking before sliding his hand up her bare thigh.

I crumpled the flimsy paper without realizing what I was doing. God, I wanted to hate Cade. Wanted to wish him dead. Wanted to hate him so much that I would do something just as hurtful back to him.

No, I didn't.

I wanted to not feel anything for him at all. That's what I wanted. I wanted not to care. I wanted not to notice. I wanted to not be aware of every move he made in his room down the hall from mine. Wanted to not be counting the minutes of the two and a half weeks that had passed since he'd said *don't* and then kissed the air out of my lungs and made me light enough to fly.

He'd barely looked at me since then. Except times like now, when he would throw his relationship with Amelia in my face. Every time I saw him at school these days, he was with her. Holding her hand in the school cafe. Laughing with her in the hallways. Feeling her up in the library during study hall when he was supposed to be in Physics.

Well, I'd gotten the message. Loud and clear. He'd had a moment with me, but that's all it was. Anything more was too big of a risk, and I understood that better than anyone what that risk would cost. I wasn't worth that. I would never be worth that.

I wiped a tear and threw the crumpled program to the ground, then put my energy into applauding the solo modern dance routine from Isla Perez, hoping anyone who saw me would think I'd been moved by her performance. Who knew that I could still feel things? I'd thought I'd taught myself to bury any emotions. So close to getting out of this hellhole—five months before my eighteenth birthday and graduation—and *this* was when my heart started to beat again?

*Not fair, God. Not fucking fair.*

"Hey, Julsianna."

I didn't have to look up to see that it was Antoine Birch slipping into the empty seat at my side. Even if I didn't recognize his voice, he was the only person who called me that nickname. I'd liked it for a hot minute back in eighth grade when I thought it meant I was special to him, but as soon as I realized it was code for *I have something for you in my pants*, that liking had worn off.

I especially hated it after hearing Cade's name for me. Maybe the only difference was how I felt for the boy who'd said it, but I didn't think that was all there was to it. *Jolie* came all by itself, with no attachments. It felt more like a gift than a bribe. It was an invitation to be something more than I was. Someone different.

Julsianna was just an invitation to get on my knees.

As the applause died down, and Ms. Stacey's Advanced Drama Class took the stage to perform a scene, I resisted the urge to tell Birch that I wasn't in the mood for him. That wasn't something Julianna would say. That was something Jolie would say, and as much as I wanted to be, that wasn't who I was yet. She was still just a seedling buried under my skin, waiting for the right season to bloom.

"What's up?" I whispered instead.

He leaned close enough that I could feel his breath tickle my ear. "This is bo-ring. Don't you think?"

I shrugged. To be honest, I'd barely been paying attention, and the show I was watching might have been devastating, but it definitely wasn't boring. Involuntarily, I slid my eyes back to Cade and Amelia. This time he wasn't watching me, and now she was on his lap, her legs spread slightly, his hand under her skirt.

The seedling inside me let out a string of curse words. Jolie, it seemed, had quite a mouth.

Biting down on the inside of my lip, I brought my ankle up to my opposite knee, facing away from Birch so he wouldn't be able to see my artwork, and took my pen to the bottom of my Mary Jane.

**I Hate. Amelia. Lu.**

I was too resentful to keep myself from using her name. Too consumed with rage to worry about what I'd say if my father discovered it. I'd have to pretend I was racist or something since he'd never believe anyone could hate Amelia. I couldn't ever let him guess the real reason.

"I swear the drama class does this *Steel Magnolias* scene every goddamn year," Birch said. "I think I have it memorized."

"Not many scenes with lots of characters, I guess." I doubted he'd paid enough attention to it any of the years prior to learn a single line, let alone memorize it, but that was Jolie who was contradicting him.

He let a good three minutes go by before saying anything else. "'...I've just been in a very bad mood for forty years!'" He laughed, quoting one of the more infamous lines from the scene.

I guess he did know the show after all.

I pretended to laugh. I was quite good at smiling while dying inside. I really should have been on that stage. If my father wasn't so controlling of all my extracurricular activities, maybe I would have.

"Whatcha drawing?" Birch stretched his arm on the seat behind me. Casually. Like he was just trying to make it easier to talk to me without disturbing the whole audience.

I wasn't stupid.

"Just doodling." I dropped my pen in my lap and crossed my legs, instinctively hiding what was between my thighs as well as what was on my shoe.

Like the single-minded sex addict that he was, he seemed to think I was flirting. He brought his hand up from the chair back to tickle along my neck.

My whole body tensed.

He ignored the cues and brought his opposite hand to my knee. "You should let me doodle." His whisper had grown husky. "My fingers are amazing at...doodling."

I knew how to get him to leave me alone. The same trick I used every other time he started to come on to me. By now, I had a feeling that he only offered to take care of me first because he knew I'd push his hand away and suck him off instead.

Not for the first time, I considered that it didn't have to be one or the other. It could be both. It could be neither. I could say no to all of it.

It was possible I didn't know how to say no. It had been so long since I'd actually tried it. It had been so long since I'd cared about saying no. There were benefits to being the girl who'd put out. There was satisfaction in getting away with something my father abhorred. I was careful about where and when I performed, and the boys definitely weren't going to confess to him.

And it made me feel wanted.

I knew that wasn't real—they wanted any hand around their cocks. They didn't care whose face the lips were attached to. They didn't want *me*.

But it felt close enough to real for me to accept it. To crave it, even.

And most days I was pretty sure it was all I was good for, so why not be the best that I could be?

It would be easy enough right now, in the dark. My father, preoccupied with dealing with the troublemakers in his office. I could slip my hand into his khakis and get him off. Birch was an early releaser. It wouldn't take more than five minutes. Maybe less since, knowing him, he'd probably find the whole public thing too hot to hold out.

It could even be satisfying for me, if I convinced myself that Cade would look down the aisle and see. If I could believe he'd care. I could fantasize his jealousy into something real instead of just a projection of what I felt inside.

"What do you say, Julsianna?" His fingertips had reached the elastic band of my panties.

I pushed his hand away. "Antoine..." I scolded in a tone that was more flirty than reprimand.

He took my hand with his. "Then maybe *you* could doodle instead." He placed my palm on the bulge at his crotch and helped me rub him. "You know what I like."

He liked what they all liked.

The same thing.

No commitments, no obligations in return.

Except Cade. I kept offering myself to him, and he hadn't taken. Was it possible he cared about me for more than just that? Or did he really not care enough to take the chance?

Back to that, always back to him. And I couldn't know what he thought or what he wanted because he wouldn't talk to me. All I could know was myself, and even if I meant nothing to Cade, there was Jolie now. He'd made her real inside me, and Jolie was faithful, if not to Cade, then to herself.

Jolie didn't want to be the school boy toy anymore.

Jolie knew how to say no.

Quietly, though, since she wasn't real enough yet to make a scene. "This isn't the best idea," I whispered, trying to extricate my hand from under his.

He clamped down on it harder, forbidding my escape. "That's what makes it such a fun idea. Come on. You can use my sweater to clean up if you don't want to use your mouth."

My stomach turned rock hard. I didn't want to fight him. *Please, don't make me have to fight him.* "I really don't want to right now, Birch."

"I'll be fast." He unzipped his pants with his free hand, not bothering with the button, and pulled out his dick from the hole in his boxers. "I'm already super hard. Feel it."

"No," I hissed, surprising myself. "No," I said again, stronger, when he tried to force my hand around his girth.

"Don't be like this, Juls. Don't play like you're suddenly a prude."

"I don't. Want. To." I glared hard at him, as though my stare could stand up to his strength.

"Why are you being such a bitch right now? I'm not even asking you to suck me. Just give me a little tug."

I was about to put my shoulder into pushing him away when suddenly he wasn't there anymore to push.

"She said no, you asshole!" Cade had lifted him out of his chair and was holding him by the scruff of his shirt, his expression brutal.

It was an unusual look on Cade. He was generally

somber, but he wasn't a bully. And if anyone were to place bets, odds would probably go to Birch who was practiced at being a bully.

From my vantage point, though, where I could clearly see the look in his eyes—my money was on Cade all the way.

"Ah, I get it. Big brother's got dibs on you now, does he?" Birch didn't seem to have the same perspective I did.

Not until Cade's fist landed squarely in his face. With the sound of skin smacking against skin, I realized the stage had gotten awfully quiet.

The attention of everyone in the auditorium had turned to us.

Panic rushed through me—panic for Cade—as a familiar voice cut through the silence. "What the hell is going on here? Birch. Warren. In the hall."

My father had returned. *Fuck, fuck, fuck.*

Birch yanked himself away from Cade's grasp and wiped his bloody nose with the back of his sleeve. "I didn't do shit," he said, as he walked past me down the aisle, pleading his case while he used his sweater to help stop the bleeding. "He just hit me out of the blue. He's trouble, Headmaster Stark. You know he is."

It was absolute bullshit but an obvious line of defense. Everyone in the school knew how often Cade was in my father's office.

Cade didn't look at me as he followed after. He also didn't say a word.

"Ms. Stacey," Dad bellowed. "Tell your students to

pick up where they left off." He opened the door to the auditorium and waited for the two boys to follow after.

I exchanged a glance with Amelia, who was sitting back in her own chair and appeared to want to stay out of the whole business. For the first time since I'd met her, though, her expression wasn't friendly. She looked very much like she was about to start writing **I hate Julianna Stark** on the bottom of her shoes.

I couldn't worry about her right now. What mattered was standing up for Cade.

Rushing out, I caught up with them still in the hall. "Cade was defending me, Daddy," I called out.

He stopped to throw me a look that I knew very well, one that told me to stay the fuck out of it or pay the consequences.

I was trained to step down with that look.

It took willpower that I didn't know I had to override that instinct. "Birch was getting handsy," I insisted.

And I swallowed. Because there was no way that my father wouldn't think that was my fault. There was no way that he would believe his daughter over the claims of one of the most important students in his student body.

"Now this dick is corrupting your daughter too," Birch said, with as much drama as the actors on the stage we'd just left, his words muffled through the sweater still pressed to his nose. "Un-fucking-believable. You're not going to let him get away with that, Headmaster Stark, are you? My dad will be very disappointed."

"Watch your mouth, Birch." But my father was

already talking softer to him. There was no way he was going to be punished for anything.

"She's telling the truth," a voice interrupted from behind me. "Antoine was trying to get Julianna to do something she didn't want to do."

Amelia had followed me out after all. Like I needed more reasons to feel guilty for hating her.

My father might be able to ignore what I said or what Cade said—he hadn't said anything, apparently aware that nothing he said would matter—but he couldn't just disregard another paying student's accusations. Could he?

"I didn't do—!"

"That's enough, Birch." My father's eyes scanned us one by one, the fury behind them growing as he evaluated his options.

I could imagine what he wanted from me. *It's no big deal*, he wanted me to say. Wanted me to save him from having to severely discipline a high-profile student.

It would be better for me to say it. I was already going to get in trouble for "provoking" Birch's advances. He might cut me a break if I took back the accusation now.

All I cared about was what helped Cade. And I honestly didn't know what that was, so I stayed silent.

Cade saw an opportunity to help himself. "Just looking out for my sister, sir," he said, looking directly at me with an expression that said there was no way in hell he thought of me as his sister.

My heart stuttered in my chest.

"Regardless," my father said after a beat. "You can't punch other students. That's behavior that should result in expulsion."

"Exactly," Birch said.

"Shut up, Antoine. If you don't want to face expulsion yourself, you'll take what you got as punishment and leave it at that."

So he'd get away with it. Of course, he would.

"Thank you, ladies," my father continued, dismissing us. "Please return to the assembly. I'll take care of it from here." He turned to Birch. "Get yourself cleaned up." Then to Cade. "My office."

I prayed Cade's punishment wasn't terrible. It couldn't be, could it? He couldn't risk Amelia Lu running home to her parents and complaining about injustice, and the best way to avoid that would be a slap on the wrist.

One look at Cade said he didn't share my optimism. But he stared at me for long seconds, then whispered, "Worth it," before following my father down the hall.

# FOURTEEN

## CADE

I TURNED OFF THE WATER, grabbed a towel from the stack outside the boy's shower, and tied it around my waist. It had taken fifteen minutes before my fingers and nose didn't feel frostbitten from being outside, but all in all, it had been the easiest punishment Stark had ever given me. I would hands down choose an hour running six miles versus five minutes with the whip, any day, no matter the toll to my body.

While the physical pain had been more tolerable, I was still wrestling with what it had done to my psyche. I'd thought I'd already seen the worst of my stepfather, or imagined it, and yet I was still somehow surprised by his reaction to today's events.

I'd known he was a monster.

But even monsters protected their own children, didn't they?

Guess I'd been wrong because all Birch had gotten

was what I'd given him, and in the end, that wasn't that much. I'd hit him hard enough to bleed, but the nurse had come into Stark's office while I'd been in there and told him his nose hadn't been broken. Disappointing. He should have been expelled for assault. He should have been in jail for what he'd tried to do to his daughter.

I would have killed the guy if Jolie was in any way mine.

I wasn't sure I wouldn't have killed him today if I hadn't been stopped. I sure fucking wanted to.

I shook my head of the thought, drops of water splattering from my hair to the tile, then walked out of the shower area toward the lockers.

Despite all the hard surfaces, the locker room was strangely peaceful when it wasn't filled with an entire gym class. I was actually glad Stark had suggested I clean up there after my run instead of going home. Of course, he'd passed it off as doing me a favor, and I was sure he'd lord it over me anytime he got a chance. How he'd gone soft on me. How there was no other student who could get away with violence and still be enrolled. How he'd have to think up some way to explain his leniency to Birch's parents.

He definitely wasn't done punishing me for this.

I forced myself not to dwell on it. It was no good wasting the present by worrying about what he'd do to me tomorrow, and honestly, he'd find something to do to me whether he thought I deserved it or not.

But when I wasn't thinking about what cruelty might

come next, my head went in an even worse direction
—Jolie.

*Jolie, Jolie, Jolie.* I didn't even think of her as Julianna
anymore. Ever since that kiss, it was like she'd changed in
my head, and there was no way to change her back. I
knew too much about her and couldn't unknow it. I knew
how good I could be to her. I knew how good she could
be to me, and it drove me insane knowing how bad it
would be for both of us if we tried to get together.

I couldn't have her. That was the hard reality. It
could not happen between us.

And yet she was always on my mind. From morning
to night. My thoughts ranged from the innocent to wildly
dirty. I wondered what she was thinking when I sat
across from her at dinner. I imagined what she'd say if we
had a stolen moment together. It was Jolie's face I
pictured when I fucked Amelia. Jolie's name that sat on
the tip of my tongue when I whacked off in my bed at
night.

The one girl I shouldn't want, and I didn't want
anything in the world but her.

I saw her as soon as I turned down the first row of
lockers, sitting on the bench between them. As if I'd
conjured her up from a fantasy that had just been
forming in the back of my consciousness—just the two of
us here, me wearing only a towel, her panties on the
ground.

Fuck, I was getting hard just from her presence.

This was the reason she and I could never be alone
together. Why I'd worked so hard over the last couple of

weeks to be sure we never were. Why I was in deep shit for being as happy to see her as I was cautious.

I forced myself to lean into caution. "You shouldn't be here." I didn't even want to know why she was there, because whatever reason she had, it was trouble.

"I had to be sure you were okay," she said, standing up, and I wondered how long she'd been waiting. The whole time? While I'd been naked in the shower nearby?

I tried to forget that I was practically naked now. "I'm fine. Now leave."

"He didn't—?" She cut herself off, and I could tell she was trying to decide what to say. It was funny how we did that—how we danced around the words of what her father did to us, as if they were worse than the things he actually did. "It wasn't too horrible? Just the running?"

She'd been looking out for me, then. I had a feeling she did that more than she let on, and I hated that I liked it. Liked it a real whole lot.

But she didn't know I liked it. And if I kept that to myself, there wasn't any harm in answering her. Maybe it would even send her on her way. "That, and he's making me take care of the grounds over break."

She didn't bother to hide her skepticism.

"I'm sure there will be more to it," I said. "He probably didn't have enough time to deal with me the way he wanted to with it being the last day of the semester."

"I'm betting I'll have to pay for it later too."

I felt a burst of heat run through my veins. "You? He had his dick out when you said no, and you're the one who has to pay?" My hand was balled up in a fist at my side, and the only thing keeping me from slamming it into the locker was the fact that it still hurt from punching Birch in the face.

"I was thinking more because I stood up for you, but I'm sure he'll blame me for Birch too."

"That's fucked up. That's. Fucked. Up."

"I know. But you know that's how it is. Don't worry about me."

It was like asking me not to worry about how I'd breathe if the room suddenly filled up with water. I couldn't help it.

I was worried about her now. "Whatever he's planning, it's going to be worse if he catches you in here. You really need to go."

She didn't move. "He's got parents arriving now until late. He's preoccupied. He's not coming back."

There came the water, filling in around me, because if I wasn't worrying about keeping her safe from her father, then I was thinking about...

Things I shouldn't be thinking.

"Go, Jolie."

Instead, she took a step forward. "Amelia asked me to give this to you."

The note was folded into a fancy square so that it tucked into itself. She'd done this a few times, passed notes to me, and it bothered me since it made it seem like we were more than we were.

But most of her messages were about when she'd be free to hookup, and it was the best way to communicate, honestly. Even if Stark had shelled out money for me to have a phone like the kids at his school, I wouldn't have wanted any records of correspondence. A note could be burned. A text could be read.

So even though this was standard between us, I had a feeling the tone of this note was different.

I took it from Jolie's hand, careful not to show her effect on me when my fingers touched her skin, but once I had it, I didn't know what to do with it. It wasn't like I had pockets, and reading it in front of Jolie felt awkward.

Then again, she might have already read it.

I opened it and scanned it quickly.

**It's okay. I won't tell. If you need something from me, I'll help.**

**See you after the holiday.**

**xx**

There wasn't any question what Amelia was referring to, and while I trusted her and felt relieved that she'd keep it hushed, having my secret called out—having it confirmed outside of me—made this thing I felt for Jolie real. Made it harder to put away and ignore.

"I think Amelia thinks..." Jolie was still standing there. Studying me.

"Thinks *what*?" I didn't know why I was daring her like this. Daring her to be bold and say the thing that shouldn't be said. I could feel my heart racing, like I'd just finished running the six miles instead of twenty minutes ago.

"Thinks there's something going on between us."

"Did you read it?" I asked angrily, though I wasn't quite sure why.

"I didn't have to."

Whatever she thought it said—whatever she thought it meant—she didn't *know*. And that meant I still had a chance to hide the elephant in the room. Could I really be surprised that Amelia had noticed? I'd been too obvious—always reaching for her as soon as Jolie showed up. Always letting her go as soon as Jolie left.

And today, I'd had my hands up Amelia's skirt, but my attention had been one hundred percent down the aisle. Thankfully. Or I might not have stopped Birch before he took advantage of her.

I really owed Amelia a fucking apology.

But shitty as it was, I was not thinking about Amelia right now.

I was thinking about Jolie's tongue sweeping across her bottom lip, and the way her throat moved when she swallowed, and how dark her eyes had gotten in the well-lit locker room, and how my skin was still damp and only a dropped towel away from being completely exposed.

I forced myself to look away. "Well, there isn't, so no big deal."

"Don't do that," she said, pulling my gaze back. The corners of her mouth had turned down, serious to a point I'd never seen. Scolding and imploring all at once. "We have to lie to everyone all the time, but I can't stand it if you lie to me."

The hair stood up on the back of my neck and down my arms, and I was suddenly aware how thin my defenses were, how she'd gotten behind walls I'd put up without realizing.

And fuck. I wanted her there, inside the fortress, with me.

But I wanted her safe, more. "I don't know what you're talking about."

"You do. You stood up for me."

"I would have stood up for anyone."

"You wouldn't have noticed it was happening if it was just anyone. Stop lying. Be honest with me."

She'd closed the distance between us, and I was so weak from the power of her that I couldn't even make myself step away. "Stop it. Stop this."

Her eyes sparkled with unshed tears. "I can't. Not any more than you can. It takes strength that I don't have to keep fighting it."

Strength I didn't have either.

"Jolie..." I was practically begging now, and I wasn't even sure anymore what I was begging for. For her to go? For her to stay?

"Please, Cade." She was begging too, and my eyes couldn't move from her lips.

I was being ripped apart, my head commanding me to step back, my heart wanting to lean forward. Stretching me beyond capacity to be stretched.

Barely able to keep my hands at my sides, frustration erupted from me. "What do you want from me?"

"I want you to love me!"

Instantly, Amelia's note fell to the ground, and my hands came up to grip her shoulders and push her into the row of lockers. "I do," I growled, unable to hold back the truth. "I already fucking do."

I hadn't even said it to myself, but with the words in the air, my chest released, and I felt the peace of surrender, the wild war that I'd been fighting finally at its end. I *did* love her, and it had been hard to admit or recognize, not only because of the odds against us, but because I hadn't ever really loved anyone before, and I had no idea what it was.

Now though, in this moment, there was no doubt. It was *this*. It *had* to be this. It was always and forever only going to be this.

In a blink, my lips were on hers, kissing her softly, trying to savor her. Trying to *show* her how I felt, that my love was patient and sweet and slow, nothing like what she'd been shown all her life from her devil of a dad.

But now that I was reconnected to her, I couldn't hold back, and quickly I was ravaging her, eating her up like the starving man that I was. My mouth wanted to know every part of hers, my tongue wanted to make its mark, wanted to claim her as mine. I didn't even notice my hands move from her shoulders until they were under her skirt, gripping her ass, pulling her pelvis against the hard ache between my legs.

Her hands were harder to lose track of. My skin burned everywhere she touched, leaving a trail of fire as her fingers skated down my torso to my waist, and even though alarm bells screamed in my head the whole time, it wasn't until I felt the towel loosening that I had the sense to pull myself together.

I brought my hand to her wrist to stop her. "That isn't the way I love you."

Hurt flashed across her mossy-blue eyes. "You don't want—"

"No, I do. I really fucking do." I wanted her more than I'd wanted anything, and I'd said it wrong. "I mean, I don't need this to love you."

"I know." She blinked at me like she might cry. "But I think I need this to know that you do."

She leaned forward and captured my mouth with hers, tugging me to her with a hand behind my neck. Her other hand had gotten beneath the barely-hanging-on towel, and with her fingers wrapped around my throbbing cock, it was extremely difficult to remember what was wrong with this. To hell that she was my stepsister—I couldn't fucking care less about that—but it was wrong to take what she was giving. She was an abused girl, and as little as I knew about life, I did know that I wanted to be different for her. I didn't want to be the person who required something from her. I didn't want her to think she had to earn me when the reality was there was nothing I could ever do that would make me worthy of her.

But her lips.

And her hand.

And the peek of her breasts as I unbuttoned her shirt and kissed my way down her chest.

And the dampness of her panties on my thigh that had somehow made its way between her legs.

There was no going back from what we'd started.

With a growl in the back of my throat, I pushed her panties down, letting them fall to her ankles before lifting her up, bracing her against the locker, which I doubted felt very good, but I couldn't seem to make myself care. Much as I wanted slow and sweet with her, this was what this love was going to be between us— rough and troubled and uncomfortable. It wasn't my choice to make. It was one that had been made for us— our lives, our circumstances—but it didn't make it any less beautiful, and all I could do was embrace it.

The towel no longer between us, she freed one foot from her panties and they dangled around the other as she wrapped her legs around me, pressing her heat against my cock. I tilted my hips up, sliding my length up and down along her slit, and grew immediately harder. She was so fucking wet. Dripping, like I'd already given her an orgasm.

On my next glide down, she tipped her pelvis forward and used her hand to guide me where she wanted me. "I need you here." Her voice was low yet heavy. "Inside."

My tip was already at her core, pushing in slightly, then pulling out. Teasing, which wasn't my intent. I was trying to convince myself to be smart. I was already an idiot for letting us get this far, but this right here was where I had to pause and think.

She sensed my hesitation. "I'm not a virgin," she said tentatively.

I'd tried not to let myself wonder, but when I did, I'd assumed she wasn't. Not with what I'd known she did with other guys. I was jealous, of course, but that wasn't why I'd hesitated. "I don't have a condom."

Surprisingly, she seemed relieved.

"Did you think I cared about that?" I couldn't keep myself from pushing my tip back inside her. She felt too good. Too hot. Too perfect.

"I didn't...I didn't know. I was afraid—"

I cut her off with a kiss. "It doesn't matter who you've been with before. I only care that you're with me now."

She tilted her hips again, drawing me deeper inside her, and I moaned. "Mmm, fuck. It doesn't change the fact that I don't want to knock you up."

"Pull out." She pushed forward, until I was practically spearing her completely. "I need you. I trust you."

I wasn't sure I trusted myself. I'd never been bare inside a girl. When I hadn't had condoms, I hadn't gone inside. It was my firm rule. There were other ways to get a release.

But all the rules were out the window with Jolie.

Against my better judgment, I told my head to shut the fuck up and thrust all the way in. "God, that's so good. You feel so good."

I hammered into her, setting a brisk though unsteady tempo, wishing I didn't need both hands around her to keep her up so that I could rub her clit and make it good for her too. I made sure to angle her against me instead, so that my pelvic bone knocked against her, hoping that would get her the friction she needed.

I couldn't think about it too much beyond that. I needed all my concentration to be sure I didn't accidentally come inside her. When she locked her ankles behind my back, making her feel even tighter, I was sure I wasn't going to last long. I could make myself think about her father (I didn't), and I probably would have been just as helpless.

It wasn't just the way it felt to be bare inside her that had me so turned on, though she did feel incredible. Like nothing else I'd ever known. It was also how much I'd wanted her. How I'd been denying her. That want had built up inside me. I was a powder keg giving off sparks. I was already so close to exploding before I'd entered her.

But mostly, the thing that had me so close to the edge was the pressure in my chest, a tightening that had nothing to do with sex and all to do with how I felt about her. She was the only star in a very dark night. She was a light that seemed to shine only on me, and the heat of that light—the fire of her attention—had me burning up from head to toe. My blood was blazing like a line of gasoline caught flame, and when her pussy clamped down around me, I knew I was a goner.

More abruptly than I intended, I set her down, pulling out as I did. Breathing heavily, I pressed my forehead to hers. She hadn't finished. It felt selfish to finish myself off like this.

But before even a handful of seconds had passed, her hand was wrapped around me again, tugging on my head while she kissed me. And forget about thinking about her pleasure. I was seeing fireworks, the base of my spine tingling as tiny rockets shot from my cock up and down my nervous system. Erupting wasn't a strong enough word for what was happening inside me. I was exploding. I was destroyed.

I let out a stuttering groan, coming all over her hand in ribbon-like spurts.

It seemed to take a lifetime before I'd caught my breath.

Her too, I realized when I could finally see straight again, her panting synced with mine. As my vision cleared, my head did too, and the enormity of what had transpired hit me like a wrecking ball.

I backed away from her quickly, then ran my hand through my hair that was as wet now from sweat as from the shower.

Jolie's back straightened against the locker, and she pierced me with a desperate stare. "Don't you dare pull away from me."

The thought had crossed my mind.

Briefly.

"No chance," I said honestly. Bravely. "You're wrapped around me like an anchor." I picked up my towel from the floor and cleaned off her hand before bending to wipe between her legs. I already regretted not spending more time down there. I wanted to fuck her with my fingers. I needed to fuck her with my mouth.

She pulled me back up to a standing position. "An anchor, huh? I go down, you go down?"

I'd meant it to be romantic, but I chuckled. She was probably more on point. "Sink or swim. We're doing it together."

Her breath shuddered. "Promise? You won't try to push me away again?"

I brushed my lips across hers. "Promise." I kissed her for real then, feeling the twin desires already wrestling inside me, the one that wanted to keep her safe. The other that wanted to keep her mine.

I'd have to find a way to do both because I couldn't give her up now. I was too selfish. I needed her to keep me from going insane.

Right now, though, while I was thinking rationally, I made myself do the smart thing. "But I need you to go. I know you said your father is preoccupied, but there are other people who could catch us. We have to be more careful than this."

"I know. You're right." She didn't let go of me when I let go of her.

"Jolie," I nudged.

"I love you," she said. "I didn't say it back."

I hadn't had time to wonder about it. I was still processing the fact that I loved her, and without having time to work it all out, I was already sure it was independent of how she felt about me.

But God, it felt good to know she felt the same.

I started to reach for her again and stopped myself before I got lost in another kiss. "Tonight. After your father's asleep."

"He locks me in with a key," she reminded me. "You can't get in any easier than I can get out."

Still high from the orgasm and from her loving me, I

didn't feel the intensity of rage I usually felt when I thought about how much I hated that man.

Besides, I had another plan. "Don't worry about that. I'll get to you." *I'll always get to you.*

She didn't know it yet, but that was a promise too.

# FIFTEEN
## JOLIE

I WAS CONCENTRATING SO hard on my bedroom door, listening for any sound on the other side, that the knock on my window made me jump.

Buzzing with excitement, I crawled across my mattress, threw back the curtain, and shoved the window up. It was the same kind we had throughout the second floor, the kind that pushed up with no screen, but unlike Cade's, the only way to the roof from mine was up.

My stomach was already in knots before I stuck my head out and looked above me to find Cade on his stomach. "Oh my God, you're going to fall!"

He grinned, half reassuring, half amused. "I won't. Just move out of the way so I can swing in."

"Oh no. No freaking way." I was so emphatic, I'd forgotten to be quiet. I clapped a hand over my mouth and listened for any sounds behind me before whisper-shouting. "Don't even think about it."

This time he actually laughed, and I realized I didn't ever remember hearing him laugh before. It mesmerized me so much that this time when he told me to move away, I did.

A tense thirty seconds later, he'd swung himself around, dropped his toes to the windowsill, then worked his way in, feet first.

After a surprised beat, I knelt on the bed and helped him—or pretended to help him. If he fell, it wasn't like I had the strength to pull him back up, but having something to do made me feel calmer, and besides, I really liked touching him.

I shut the window as soon as he was in, not wanting to let too much cold air in, then sat back, my legs curled under me, and stared at him.

*Holy shit.*

Cade was in my room.

The door was locked from the outside, and Cade was in my room, and my father didn't know, and I'd never been happier.

Until he reached his hand out and cupped the side of my face, which made me even happier.

I was also a nervous wreck. "You could have killed yourself."

"Doing that? Piece of cake."

"You should have come in the bathroom window." It faced the side of the house instead of the back, and the roof was easily accessible. I'd never climbed out that way because I was not too big of a fan of heights, but I was willing to try it when it was warmer.

"Too narrow for my shoulders," he said with certainty.

Which made me realize... "You've thought about this before. About sneaking in my room."

For half a second, I thought he was going to deny it. "All the fucking time."

My heart flipped, and I blushed. It could have been meant as a sweet comment or a dirty one, and instead of choosing which he'd meant, my body reacted to both.

Holy shit, Cade was in my room, and he was going to do sweet and dirty things to me real soon. Wildly dirty, maybe even.

Instinctively, I looked to my door. I'd never been granted happiness in my life without my father lurking in the shadows, ready to take it away.

Cade followed my line of vision. "He already came by, didn't he? I swear I heard him go downstairs before I came over."

"He did, but we should have a sign in the future. If you had knocked when he was in here..." My stomach tightened, thinking about the possibility of him coming over too soon.

"Next time, open the window a crack as soon as he leaves. I won't knock unless it's open."

I nodded, but I was still staring at the door. It was after midnight, and he'd already done his check-in, but I couldn't help worrying it would be one of those nights where Dad decided he wanted to say good night to me again. It was rare, but not out of the question. Especially if he'd punished me earlier in the day. He seemed to think an extra visit to my room could make up for whatever cruelty he'd dispensed.

"You think he might come back?" Well, now I was only thinking about my upper arm since his hand was stroking my skin there. "Will you feel better if we move the dresser in front of the door?"

It wasn't a very heavy dresser and wouldn't stop anyone for long, but any extra barrier seemed like a good idea.

Either he felt the same or sensed how I felt because he stood up to move it before I'd answered. I jumped up to join him, and together we pushed the dresser until it hit the doorknob and couldn't go any farther.

Once it was in place, Cade put his hand on the doorknob and turned it, testing it. "He really, really locks you in."

I nodded. I'd had years to get used to being treated like a possession more than a person. A lifetime trained to be the model daughter, only existing for my father's needs and nothing else. It had been a long time since I'd tried to remember that most children weren't treated this way, and though I had a feeling Cade's life hadn't been "normal" either, I also knew my father had to be a new kind of devil.

"How do we live like this?" he asked, and it was a rhetorical question, but I knew that the answer was that we didn't.

At least, I hadn't. I hadn't lived. I hadn't felt like I'd lived, anyway. Not until this year. Not until Cade.

And now it was just the two of us, alone in my room,

and even after he'd been inside me only hours before, I suddenly felt shy. "Hi," I said.

"Hi," he said back.

He stood there and looked at me then, really looked at me, and with the moonlight coming into the room, I could see his eyes move down my body. Could tell when he noticed my nipples budding through my nightgown. Watched as he adjusted the crotch of his jeans.

"Are you cold?" But he was smirking, like he already knew the answer.

"I'm not cold." Immediately, I regretted my response. If I were better at being flirty or seductive, I'd have said something witty, told him I was freezing and needed him to warm me up.

It must not have mattered that I'd said something so lame because he prowled over to me anyway, like I was exactly as tempting as I wanted to be to him. He cupped my cheeks with his hands and moved his mouth lightly over my face, keeping his lips only a breath away. "There are so many things I want to do to you."

I closed my eyes, waiting for his kiss. "What kinds of things?" I could barely hear my whisper above my pounding heart.

"So many terrible naughty things that I fantasized about doing all those times I thought about sneaking in your window. It's going to take a lot of restraint not to do them all to you tonight."

"But you could do at least some of them."

"Maybe one."

My eyes flew open. "Only one?"

He chuckled, then kissed me quickly on the lips. "I'm serious about there being more than fucking between us." He took my hand and tugged me toward the bed. "Let's talk."

"We've had months of the 'more' between us. I think we deserve some time playing catch-up on the fucking." It wasn't that I was particularly into sex. I'd never done it for my own enjoyment. I'd never even had an orgasm.

But I knew what to do with sex. I knew how to use it to be worth noticing. I knew how to exchange it for a favor. I knew how it could make a boy say nice things.

I didn't know how to make a boy say nice things without it.

I didn't know how to be with a boy without it.

Yet here I was, climbing onto my bed with a boy who emphatically didn't want to just fuck.

I didn't know if I felt like flying or throwing up.

Cade propped himself up against the wall next to the window, then pulled me into him and wrapped an arm around me. "You're so tense," he said, his hand caressing my arm again. Goosebumps peppered across my skin in its wake. "Still worried we'll be caught?"

"I don't know."

His lips pressed against my temple. "You said no lying. Are you really that scared of letting me hold you?"

*Yes.*

But it was getting easier as the seconds passed, especially since I was facing away from him. "I guess it's not so bad. I just don't know what to talk about."

"Anything you want. Or you don't have to say anything, if you'd rather."

Both options sounded awkward.

But there was something I wanted to know. "What did Amelia's note say?"

"You said you already knew."

I hadn't read it. I'd wanted to, but I'd stopped myself, hoping that Cade would tell me himself. Even if he didn't, I'd seen the look in her eyes when she'd handed it to me. She knew whatever they had was over.

"I guess I don't care so much about what her note said. I care more about your reaction."

He pulled away so he could look at me. "Now I really need to hear what you thought it said."

"She broke up with you?" My voice squeaked, and now that I'd said it out loud, I was really afraid that it wasn't true.

"I guess she did? There wasn't anything to break up. She knew I wasn't into her. She just didn't know why until today."

"You really weren't into her?"

"Worse. I was using her. Do you think the worst of me now?"

"Using her to...?"

"To keep everyone from figuring out how I feel about you." A mountain fell off my shoulders. I'd told myself I didn't care what he felt for her, but it was a lie. I cared a lot. Especially since I was pretty sure they'd actually been fucking. It was a relief to know it had been the charade I'd thought it had been.

And I really loved hearing him talk about his feelings for me. It was probably going to take some time before I truly believed it, so I was glad he wasn't keeping it inside like a secret that only had to be admitted once.

"I guess it is more than my father who can't know," I said, realizing for the first time what it would look like to others. "People would probably think it's sick."

"Or kinky."

I let out a snort. Then second-guessed his meaning. "Is that what you think—?"

He cut me off with a kiss. "You know what we are. Better than I do, maybe. And I've already told you this isn't about sex for me. Isn't *just* about sex."

I wrapped my arms around him, and his hand grazed my breast as it skated down my ribs, making me very eager to climb on his lap.

Just as I was heating up, he slowed things down. "I think Amelia offered to help be our cover. I'll let that be your decision. Either way, even if I pretend to be with her, I promise I won't be with her again. Not like this."

I loved that he thought about my feelings. Loved that he was sure enough about me to make promises.

But he was still new to the compromises that had to be made on behalf of my father, and I didn't want to tell him that there were some promises that couldn't be made, but instead I said thank you and rested back into his arms, pressing my cheek against his chest.

We sat quietly for several minutes, his hand tracing up and down my arm, and soon I felt my body relaxing, the rock in my stomach lightening, and I could no longer hear my heartbeat racing in my ears.

I could hear his heartbeat, though, steady under my ear. It was so steady, I almost thought he'd fallen asleep.

Then he asked, "What happened after dinner?"

The bowling ball in my stomach returned. As I'd suspected I would be, I'd been called to my father's office. In all honesty, it had been a pretty typical punishment. Nothing I couldn't handle.

I really hated bringing that into this room though. I wanted Cade all to myself. "Do we have to talk about my father?"

I could feel him sigh underneath me. "No. Not if you don't want to. But I think you've never been able to talk to anyone about him, and I don't want you to have to carry that alone anymore."

But I'd carried it alone so long. I didn't know how to share it. I couldn't imagine letting someone else have to burden it with me, even though I was well aware that Cade already did share it with me, whether we talked about it or not.

I took a deep breath and tested what it felt to tell him...something. "He said he didn't believe Birch did anything that I didn't ask for, and if I got myself pregnant, I was out of here."

"In that case, maybe I should get you pregnant."

I ignored him because I didn't think he meant it and because I knew my father didn't mean it. He would never willingly take his hooks off me. "He also said if I hadn't asked for it, well, um. I shouldn't be surprised." I cleared my throat. "Shouldn't be surprised that boys like Birch treat me that way. Because that's what whores were for."

He went stiff. "He called you that?"

I was glad I didn't have to look at him when I nodded. It only felt hard to share because my abuse was different than his. It seemed my father's favorite weapon with Cade was pain. With me, it was humiliation.

He swore under his breath, then turned me so he could look at me.

"It's okay," I said, before he could give me his pity. "I'm used to it." Calling me a whore wasn't anything new. It was the first time I'd heard *cum bucket*, however.

"It's not okay, Jolie. And I'm never going to accept your 'it's okay' because you believe it."

Something cracked inside me. Some deep part of my foundation. *No,* I wanted to insist. *Of course, I don't believe anything my father says. He lies, and he's horrible and says things just because he knows they'll hurt.*

But of course I believed him. Why else did I do the things I did with boys? I didn't want to jerk them off. I didn't want their sweaty dicks in my mouth. I didn't want their cum down my throat.

I didn't know the tears were falling until Cade was kissing them off my cheeks, whispering reassurances. "It's not true. Even if you slept with every guy in the school, it doesn't make you a whore."

"Then why do you regret having sex with me?"

He looked at me like I was insane. "Why do you think I regret it?"

"Why do you just want to sit and talk?" I was being ridiculous, but I was upset and confused, and I didn't know what I wanted.

He kept calm despite my theatrics. "I want to sit and talk because I love you. And I want you to feel loved. It doesn't mean I don't want you, and it for damn sure doesn't mean I regret it."

"I don't know how to feel loved." I was kissing him now too, but my kisses were not soothing. They were hungry and needy and desperate.

Suddenly, I was on my back, my hands stretched over my head and held down, Cade's eyes dark. "Okay, I get it," he said, hovering over me. "Talking isn't enough, but I'm not about to stick my dick in you just so you can confirm that your father's right. How about we meet each other halfway?"

I'd been so surprised by being flipped that I'd stopped crying, but my eyes were still watery. "What do you mean?"

"You let me love you. The way you need to be loved." I was already tugging his sweatshirt off when he stopped me. "There's one rule: it's all about you."

I must have looked confused because he went on. "Trust me. Can you trust me?"

I'd never trusted anyone like I trusted him. He knew most of my secrets. I'd let him into my room. Why would he need to ask?

His smile appeared, startling when he'd been so somber only a minute before. "Well, then trust me all the way. Trust me to love you, okay?"

"Uh. Okay."

"Good. Second rule—"

"I thought there was only one."

"It's a subrule related to the first one." Now he had me smiling. "I get to touch you, but you don't get to touch me."

"Oh." I was beginning to understand. "Ohhh."

And now I was feeling terrified.

I started to sit up. "I don't think I can—"

He pushed me back down. "Can you let me help you try? I'm not going to do anything you don't want me to. I'll ask first. Can I take off your nightgown?"

It was light and practically see-through, and right now it felt as heavy as a winter coat on my skin.

But taking it off meant being naked, and naked felt very unbalanced if it was only going to be me. "Will you take off your clothes too?"

He shook his head. "You already got me naked. It's my turn to see you." He bent down to tug at my nipple through the flimsy material with his lips. "I'm dying to see all of you, Jolie. You have me going crazy imagining what you look like with nothing on."

He moved his mouth to my other breast, and I moaned, "Yes." Then, just in case I wasn't clear, "Yes, you can take off my nightgown."

"If at any time you want me to stop, you just say stop, and I will." He made sure I nodded consent. Slowly, gently, he pulled the gown up my body, over my head, then pinned my arms on the bed before really looking at me.

And the sound he made then as I lay there in only my panties, and he feasted on me with his eyes...

I didn't have the vocabulary to label it. It was raw and primal. A grunt and a growl and a sigh all mixed in one. Its baseness made me feel beautiful. In a way that I was used to feeling beautiful—with my body—but also in a whole new way because I didn't think anyone had ever looked at me so thoroughly. So completely, seeing all of me. The insides along with the out. The bad as well as the good and still wanting to see more.

"You're fucking gorgeous," he said, staring at my breasts like they were diamonds. My nipples were pointed so sharply, I swore they could have cut glass, but when he licked his tongue across one, it was me who cried out.

Seriously? Just having my tit licked felt that good?

I'd never had my breasts adored, never had someone kiss them and suck on them and squeeze them and nip at them until I was wet and writhing. It was more difficult than I imagined. More than once I tried to wrestle a hand free—so I could push him away or pull him closer, I didn't know—and every time he dominated me, keeping me restrained, reminding me he'd stop if I just said stop.

I didn't want him to stop.

As strange and vulnerable as he made me feel, I wanted more.

He took his time giving it. Slowly kissing down my stomach, fucking my belly button with his tongue before moving lower.

"Can I kiss you here?" he asked, hovering just above

the very wet spot in my panties. And after I said yes, after he'd kissed me, "Can I kiss you without them on?"

"Please?" I was already about to beg him to take them off. Which had me topsy-turvy because I was a virgin at this part too—I'd never had a mouth between my legs. Never had anyone try to get me off. It was always the other way around, I was always the one giving or being taken from, and even before he had my panties down my legs, I could tell how different it was to be on the other side.

How vulnerable it made me.

How powerful. How wanted.

Even wanting them off, a rush of timidity came over me as he pulled the white flowered panties down my thighs, and I sat up suddenly.

"You're okay." He stopped, though, my underwear gathered around my knees, and of everything he'd said and done, that might have hit me hardest. "Is this okay?"

I had to look away. A deep breath later, I still couldn't look right at him.

"Did you hear something?" He was listening now, assuming that's what my problem was.

"No, I..." I had to decide quickly what to say. Another breath. "I want this. I just—"

He sat up now too. "We don't have to do this tonight."

"No! I mean, yes, we do. Because I want to. And yes, it's okay. Just, no one's done this to me before."

"Never?" He seemed surprised, and I almost wanted to ask what he thought my experience level was, but that wasn't a conversation I really wanted to have at the moment.

So I avoided the question. "I'm nervous."

He stroked the back of my calf, possibly subconsciously. "Nervous about what?"

"That I'll do it wrong."

"I'm the one who will be doing, remember?"

"Or that I won't be able to..."

"There is no end goal here." Now his caress became purposeful, up and down from my ankle to my knee. "If it feels good, it's working. If it's not, I'll stop."

Then there was the practical matter. "What if I...taste...bad?" I was glad it was too dark for him to see me blush.

"Your panties were soaked, Jolie. I could already taste you." He licked his lips. "And you tasted fucking good."

I lowered my face, trying to hide my embarrassed grin. "Okay, then. I'm ready."

I didn't lie all the way back this time. Keeping my elbows propped, I watched as he tugged my underwear off and tossed them to the floor. He kept his eyes on mine, checking in. Reading my every reaction as he gently pressed my knees apart.

I shivered when he finally tore his gaze from mine to look at what he'd uncovered. Again, his face lit up like he'd discovered buried treasure. Reverently, he ran a finger down my seam and up again.

"I'm going to lick you here," he said. "I'm going to put my tongue between your pussy lips, and then here..." He rubbed his finger around my entrance. "I'm going to lick you here. And here." He stuck it inside me, penetrating only as far as I imagined his tongue would go.

My insides clenched tight.

His finger was wet when he dragged it back along the path he'd drawn, landing at the hooded nub at the top. "I'm really going to lick this. Suck it too. Is it okay if I eat you, Jolie?"

My nod was eager.

If I thought describing what he was going to do was amazing—which I did—it was nothing compared to the actual doing. As soon as his tongue hit my skin, sparks shot through my body, awakening nerves I didn't know I had. "Ah!"

His head lifted, and I knew he was about to ask, so I beat him to it. "Still okay. *Very* okay."

He smiled briefly before—praise be—returning his tongue to my pussy. Just the swipe of it along my lips had my toes curling.

And still, my mind was a nosy bee. "Have you done this before?"

He paused to consider. The fact that he had to think was enough to make my body tighten because the answer wasn't hard. The only thing he could be considering was whether or not he should be honest.

Thankfully, he chose the truth. "Yes."

Or maybe not so thankfully because now my throat felt the hard knot of jealousy. "Amelia?"

"No." He laughed like that idea was ridiculous. "And it wouldn't matter if I had because you're the only girl

I've done this to that I loved." He licked around my hole, which felt dirty and wrong and really fucking hot. "So I really haven't done *this* before."

"Okay," I said. There seriously wasn't room for any language in my brain anymore. And also, it really was okay. More than okay. It made me happy to be his first in some way.

It made me happy that he was *my* first in this too.

He took that okay as the end of discussion, which it was, and devoted himself to his task, starting over from where he first began and leisurely running his tongue all the places he said he would. He spent several minutes at my hole before completing his sweep back up my lips.

I was quivering before he even made it to my clit.

Then when he did... Fuck. I had to lie all the way down.

I thought for a moment, as he sucked the bundle of nerves into his mouth the first time, about how I'd describe the sensation. The words that came to mind were vague. *Incredible. Heaven. Ecstasy.* It felt like little fires everywhere in my body, furnaces turned to full blast. It felt like volcanoes. It felt like...

Indescribable, really.

So I stopped trying to name it and let myself relax and just feel, and pretty soon the fires began to build and blaze, and before I knew it, my hands were wrapping into the bedsheets and my entire body was trembling. I couldn't breathe. The ball of fire inside me was too big, pressing against my lungs, growing bigger, bigger still until I thought it might overtake me.

Then it did.

My chest lifted from the bed, and pure pleasure launched through me. I was buzzing everywhere, everywhere. There wasn't a fragment of my body that was untouched by bliss—pure and intense and encompassing.

And for the first time, I had a glimpse of understanding about sex, and why people were the way they were with it, and why it was such a powerful commodity, and why so many were obsessed with taking it even when it wasn't given.

But as wonderful as it was, it was over within a minute. And though I felt more relaxed than I'd ever felt, the orgasm didn't fix anything inside of me.

"Are you okay?" Cade had stretched himself out beside me while I recovered. I could feel the bulge in his jeans pressed against my hip, but I knew he wanted me to ignore it.

For once, I did.

"I'm fantastic," I said honestly. Enlightened a bit, too.

Then I wrapped myself up in his arms and let him hold me while we talked late into the night.

# SIXTEEN
## CADE

*Present*

I JIGGLED the pick in the lock of Stark's office, grateful that Donovan had given me his jackknife pick set for the trip. It was taking me longer than I'd expected, partly because it had been a while since I'd had to engage in a task of this sort. Partly because I wasn't usually so distracted.

"It's like old times," I whispered. "Sneaking around your father's house late at night."

She laughed, making the light from the flashlight bounce. "I'm not scared enough for this to be like old times. And not naked enough."

Not right now, anyway.

I peeked over at her. Dressed in my T-shirt and

drawstring gym shorts, she might as well be naked. She had the same effect on my cock. "We could fix that last part. Would you get any satisfaction from fucking on your father's desk?"

"Ew, no." She shivered in disgust.

Honestly, I wasn't sure I would either. Too many bad memories of that room. I probably couldn't even get it up.

"We'll get our vengeance." It sounded like a promise, and I wasn't so sure she should be that assured.

But she looked so adorable with that quirky smile, wearing my clothes, and I was pretty sure I'd just gotten the last pin lifted with the wrench, so I leaned over and kissed her.

Then I opened the door.

She smiled against my lips. "That's a pretty hot trick of yours."

So apparently I could get it up.

I could wait until we were back in our room to do something about that.

I pushed the door open, then reached in and turned the light on without crossing the threshold. Instead, I stood there, looking in at the space that had been the source of so many years of nightmares. It was almost an exact duplicate of his office at school with different books lining his shelves and a window that faced south instead of west. It was smaller than I'd remembered. Better lit. More mundane.

But those changes were all about me and my grown-up, distanced perspective, because on further examination, the room seemed basically unchanged.

Jolie hadn't yet moved either. "He reorganized the books," she said, indicating she was applying the same scrutiny to the room I was.

I followed her line of sight and saw it immediately—a minor alteration, unnoticeable to anyone who hadn't spent long minutes staring at the shelves, memorizing the titles to distract from the pain. My body shuddered, remembering.

Fuck. It was terrible.

Being back here was unspeakably terrible.

I grabbed Jolie's hand in mine, and she took it quickly as though she'd been the one reaching. There was no choice but to be together in this house. Now, like then, it was the only way to survive, and I didn't question the necessity of her. Didn't think about what would happen between us when we left. Future didn't exist when you were in Stark's world. There was only the present, anchored in a shitty past. There was only living through the moment.

I pressed my palm harder against hers. "Should we?"

"Yeah," she said, straightening. Steeling herself. "Let's get this over with."

Together, we crossed into the room.

Strangely, it was just as easy to breathe as it had been out in the hall. Back then, I'd been convinced the oxygen was thinner in Stark's office. It seemed I'd been wrong.

Maybe he had to be there for the air to constrict.

Realizing it was just a space like any other made it easier to focus, and I dropped Jolie's hand and headed straight for the desk.

"Which one did you say it was in?" I asked, already tearing apart the top drawer. This had always been planned as a quick in-and-out. We needed the extra key to the cabin safe, and that was all. Planting evidence in Stark's safe was the surest strategy, and there was no reason to torture ourselves staying longer than we had to.

She didn't appear to be as motivated to be done with our task. Instead of following me to the desk, she'd crossed to the bookshelves. "*Antony and Cleopatra. All's Well That Ends Well. As You Like It.*" She paused in between each title, as though searching for the next. "They're all still here. Just not in alphabetical anymore. It looks like they're grouped by genre now."

Not finding any keys in the first drawer, I shut it and moved on to the second. "Was the key all by itself, or is it on a ring?"

"The parenting books were the ones I found particularly ironic." I heard the sound of a book being pulled off the shelf. "*Positive Discipline.* It even looks like it was actually read. There're notes in the margins."

"Let me guess—he's arguing with his methods." The second drawer was also a bust, and the bottom drawers were locked, but the sight of an external hard drive had me reconsidering our strategy.

"*Her* methods. The writer is a she, and of course, that's what the notes are. I'm surprised he even bothered reading material written by a woman."

"We could just plant the flash drive here," I said, thinking out loud.

"Not after we've been here. It's too obvious. He

could claim we planted it." She said it quickly, suggesting she'd already thought about it.

"Right, right." I would have gotten there too in a minute. And now it made me think of something else. "We should put the safe key back after so he can't say it was stolen."

Fuck. I didn't want either of us to have to come back.

"Could we get it copied tomorrow? Put it back before we ever go?"

She was sharp.

I should have been that sharp. "Good thinking." I pulled the jackknife pick from the pocket of my sweats. "You said the safe key was in a locked drawer, didn't you?"

"Bottom right, if it's in the same place it was before."

She put the book back and moved to the single book-shelf with pictures on display. A fleeting glance told me they were exactly the same photos that had been there years ago—a professional headshot of each of Stark's parents, a posed family portrait of Stark and his first wife with a toddler version of Jolie on her lap, a picture my mother had given him of me and her at my eleventh birthday party, and a formal photo from both his weddings, the first one framed and the second printed out and stuck in the corner of the glass covering the original.

"I always thought it was funny that he had these in here at all," she said. "They were always covered in dust. It wasn't like they meant anything to him, and it's not like he was putting them up to boast. No one ever came in here but us."

I'd stared at those pictures until I had every detail memorized, and I'd never thought too much about why they were there. They'd seemed incidental to me. A place he put these things that he didn't know what to do with.

I'd wondered if that's how he kept us in his mind too —relegated to a dusty shelf, never looked at, displayed exactly how he wanted us displayed. "They reminded him we were his," I said, sitting down in the chair to work on the lock.

"Was that it?" She didn't seem quite convinced.

The drawer was easier to pop than the door, and it was open almost instantly. "Got it," I said, looking up at Jolie.

She'd picked up one of the pictures from the shelf and was studying it. Now that she was holding it, I realized I didn't recognize the frame, and her earnest expression had me curious. "What is it?"

She let out a sigh. "Me. Graduation."

I knew better than to get distracted, but I needed to see it. "Show me."

She brought it over, and I stood to look at it with her. Seeing her like that, looking like she had the last time I'd seen her all those years ago, knocked the wind out of me. She looked exactly how she'd been etched in my memory —her hair a mousy brownish blonde, her face round. I could have conjured up the image of her in that cap and gown in a blink, and I hadn't even gotten to see her walk the stage. It was just another thing Stark had stolen from me. Another moment that I'd been denied.

I'd imagined it though. I'd sat in that stupid parking lot and fantasized the whole thing, waiting for her to hitch a ride with Amelia's parents and come meet up with me five miles away.

"You can tell I'd been crying," she said softly. "My eyes are puffy."

They were visibly red, and she hadn't even bothered to try to smile.

I realized what she was insinuating. "You'd already decided you weren't coming." I'd wondered for years. Wondered if she'd ever planned to come at all.

"I wasn't always not going to come," she said, reading my mind. "I'd meant it when I said I would."

And there it was—the part of the past we'd been dancing around. The thing I hadn't been able to bring myself to talk about. Because it hurt so much already, and I couldn't imagine that any reason she gave for not coming would make it better. Chances were, it would make it worse.

So I hadn't asked.

And she hadn't said.

But now it was there between us, picture proof that she'd suffered something.

I forced my eyes from the ghost in the picture to the woman at my side. "Why didn't you?"

Her lips turned down, and her eyes seemed to match the frown, but when she opened her mouth, it was another voice that spoke.

"Should have known that you weren't just stopping by for old time's sake. Should I call the cops and report a break in? There's nothing of value in there, I assure you."

Jolie jumped, and both of our gazes flew to the doorway where my mother stood in her bathrobe.

"It's not what it looks like. We were just..." As always, Jolie was quick to make amends. To smooth things over.

Fuck that. I wasn't explaining shit to my mother. "Do you even know what's in here? Have you ever taken the initiative to look for yourself? Hard drives. Locked drawers." I hadn't even gotten to the ones that held his instruments of pain.

"Your father—"

"Not my father," I corrected.

"Is the head of a prestigious school. He deals with private information all the time."

There was no use pointing out that data pertaining to Stark Academy should be kept at his school office, or that she couldn't actually know what was on all these drives unless she'd looked, which I was willing to bet she hadn't done. She'd find some way to stand by him no matter what was said, no matter what I found.

So instead, I cut to the chase. "Always so eager to defend him. To protect *him*. You're so good at it. I can't even imagine what kind of mother you would have been if you'd ever tried to use that instinct to protect *us*."

"There it is. The blame. I was waiting for it." She'd come into the office now, and if it felt like foreign territory or a line she shouldn't have crossed, she didn't show it. "You don't know shit about what I've done for you."

I let out a sardonic laugh. "I know what you *haven't* done. Frankly, that's all I need to know."

Her eyes flashed with anger, then looked at Jolie, who had slunk away to sit on the chair. Jolie had been raised to avoid conflict. I couldn't blame her for still having the urge to back away.

But that made me all the more eager to keep her out of it. "Don't look at her. She's not under his thumb anymore either. And despite not being your flesh and blood, she needed you to protect her too. We were kids, for Christ's sake."

She stared again at Jolie, pointedly this time. "You're really not going to say anything?"

I looked from one woman to the other, realizing there was an unspoken conversation happening between them that I wasn't privy to. "What? What am I missing?"

My mother folded her arms across her chest, and Jolie sighed. "Carla is the only reason I was able to get out of here, Cade. She helped me escape."

There were too many arrows in those two sentences. Too many hits to the heart. "My mother helped you? *Escape?*" The language alone shed light on what those years had been like after I'd left. He hadn't changed. Of course, he hadn't. It didn't matter that she was an adult.

So why had she fucking stayed?

There were other questions closer to the tip of my tongue. "And she knew where you were all this time?"

"No, no," Jolie insisted.

"I've had an email," my mother said.

"She had an email," Jolie confirmed.

Not only had she let my mother help her, but she'd let her stay connected as well.

This was the shit I hadn't wanted to know. This was the shit that only threatened to make painful memories hurt worse.

And the biggest sting? My mother had helped Jolie when she'd never helped me. "Fabulous. She can help you now then too."

For the second time that night, I stormed out on my mother.

This time Jolie followed sooner than she had before. She caught up with me before I'd made it to our room.

*My* room.

"Cade, please don't..." she said behind me on the stairs.

I swung around to face her at the top, sweeping my arm around her waist to catch her when my turn had taken her by surprise.

In my arms, she breathed a sigh of relief, and fuck if I didn't breathe it too. "Jolie...fuck," I said, pressing my forehead to hers, pulling strength from her touch.

"I'm sorry. I didn't know if I should tell you. I'm—"

"No, no. I'm just glad that you got out of here." It wasn't a lie. It just wasn't all the truth.

"I'm sorry," she said again. She wrapped an arm around my neck, and I could feel there was more she wanted to say, more she wanted to explain.

I just...

I couldn't hear it.

I forced myself to focus on something solid. Our plan. "I'll try to get back in there in a little while. There's still a long time before morning, and she hasn't kicked us out, so we still have a shot."

I sensed her smile before she leaned back, and I saw it. Then she held up her other hand to show me a ring of keys. "All the extra keys to the cabin. I grabbed them from the drawer while you two were arguing."

I almost laughed.

And then I did laugh. She hadn't been slinking after all. She really wasn't the girl she'd once been. She'd gotten a backbone, and I kept forgetting to see it.

I made a silent vow to recognize it more often. Then kissing her, I tugged her into our room—because as long as we were in this house together, it would be *our* room—and made another silent vow that, from now on, I was only concerned with the present.

The past needed to stay where it belonged—in the past.

# SEVENTEEN
## CADE

*Past*

"THERE ARE SO MANY FREAKING BUGS!"

I glanced up from my tire scrubbing, expecting to see Jolie swatting away mosquitos. Instead, she was frowning down at the windshield. "I never realized how dangerous cars were to insects. And what a terrible surprise that has to be, flying along, minding your own bug business and then wham! Their little guts are just caked on here, too."

I shook my head and stood up, then made sure to touch as much of her as possible as I moved her out of the way. "I'll take gut cleanup. You can take over scrubbing the tire rims."

"You mean you'll take over my dirty work for me?" She gave me the cutest little smile and blinked her eyes coyly, as if that hadn't been her plan with the comment all along.

"I wouldn't be too excited—the rims are covered in mud."

She scowled as she examined one. "How about I work on soaping up the rest of the car?"

I grinned. "Sure, sure." Honestly, she didn't have to ask. She knew I'd take all the shit parts of the task. I'd even let her sit the whole thing out if I didn't think her father would have something to say about it.

But she knelt down to work on the tire rim after all, and when I gave her a questioning eyebrow, she shrugged. "I felt guilty."

"For fuck's sake. Let me do the damn tires. Get scrubbing the hood."

She bit her lip and looked at me, wheels spinning, and I knew she wasn't thinking about whether or not to take me up on the offer but about how much she wanted to kiss me for it. Or just that she wanted to kiss me in general. It was a look I knew well. A look I often found myself giving her in return.

Four months into being a real couple, and the secrecy only got harder.

*Only eight more weeks*, I told myself. Eight weeks until graduation, and then we'd be gone. It was the mantra we'd adopted, the countdown. It was hard to imagine how we'd made it through before we had each other, because even with her, two months felt like an eternity.

Though, right at the moment, things weren't actually that bad.

Jolie echoed my thoughts. "I have to say, as far as chores go, I'd rather be scraping mud and bugs off Dad's car. It's almost not even a chore."

"I don't know. Could be better if you were wearing a bikini."

She blushed as she rolled her eyes. "You see enough of my body as it is."

"Never." Sneaking into her room every night was most definitely not enough.

But we were both in good moods, considering. The sun was out, a rare April Sunday when the temperature hit seventy, and we'd just come off of spring break. While Stark hadn't taken us anywhere, he'd gone up to his cabin for the week to hunt, which meant we'd not only had a vacation from his cruelty, but also we'd had more time to be with each other without him around, dictating our every second. We'd kept our hands to ourselves—mostly—since my mother was still around, and spent our hours reading to each other and listening to music and planning our future.

Best spring break I'd ever had, hands down.

I paused my bug scraping to watch her lift up on her tiptoes to clean the car roof. How a girl could look sexy in a white T-shirt and long swim shorts, I had no idea, but she did. Forget the bikini. I was half hard without it.

Walking past her to dip my sponge in the bucket, I glanced toward the house, wondering if anyone would see if I smacked her on the ass.

"Don't do it," she whispered.

She was so in tune with me, it was scary.

She turned her head to peer at me. "I heard Dad telling Carla he might take her away for a second honeymoon to the Bahamas. Which is a little weird since they never went on a first honeymoon."

Stark was such a tightwad with his money, I couldn't imagine him splurging on a vacation, but he'd been somewhat generous since he'd returned from his hunting trip on Friday, suggesting we get a new dishwasher and redo the driveway. "Maybe he lied about going hunting and went gambling instead. It's like he suddenly hit the jackpot."

"This car has definitely been to the cabin. And he gets like this sometimes. Splurges for a few months every couple of years. Not on us, of course. Stuff for himself. But point is, if they're going on a trip—house to ourselves." She tried to waggle her eyebrows and failed.

God, she was so adorable it hurt.

"Wait—your father's going to take a trip while school's in session?"

"No, the summer." She came flat to her feet, realization dawning on her face. We wouldn't be here this summer. "Oh." It took her a second, then she grinned.

It was strange to think of a future not tied to this hellhole, and I'd been here less than a year. I couldn't begin to understand how she felt. It was hard not to feel like her hero. We hadn't even left yet, but just knowing it was on the horizon made me feel like I'd already rescued her.

Cocky, maybe.

But I could admit she'd already rescued me too.

Her eyes suddenly focused on something behind me, and the grin disappeared. "That's for you."

Students had returned earlier that morning, but very few ever wandered all the way back here, so I already guessed who it was before I turned to see Amelia Lu standing at the edge of the property.

"Sure, Cade, I'll take over the work while you go get cozy with your girlfriend." As good as she was at hiding things, Jolie's resentment toward Amelia was obvious.

"You could come talk to her with me."

"Because it's natural for stepsisters to tag along like a third wheel," she said sarcastically. "Good thinking."

I wanted to tease her about her jealousy and then pull her into my arms and kiss her until she felt reassured, but both were off limits in the daylight. After dropping my sponge in the bucket, I took a smaller risk and playfully tugged on the back of her ponytail. "Be right back."

I jogged to the edge of the drive, Jolie's stare heavy on my back.

"Careful," Amelia said when I was close enough to hear her. "You guys look awfully cozy."

"We're washing a car together. I've barely touched her." It was easy to get defensive considering how much I knew I was holding back.

"You don't have to touch each other. You guys have googly eyes that can be seen for miles." She was teasing me, and she was warning me, all at once.

"Yeah, yeah. You're probably right." I sighed. "Is that why you're here? Checking up on us?"

"Figured I should probably come say hi to my *boyfriend* after being gone a week."

Amelia was the one person in the world who knew about me and Jolie, and no, I wasn't worried about her telling anyone. I'd been nervous about talking to her when she came back from winter break, sure that she'd guessed and intent on convincing her otherwise.

But she was too smart to buy it, and after everything, she deserved the truth. Thankfully, she'd promised to keep it hush. A few weeks later, she went a step further and offered to continue to pretend to be my girlfriend, to throw off any suspicions around campus. She had her own motivations, it turned out, since she'd moved on from booty calls with me to booty calls with the new Latin teacher and appreciated being able to use me to explain her frequent hickeys.

Jolie knew about the arrangement, of course, and appreciated Amelia for it, though she understandably didn't like it.

And I tried to pretend I didn't like how much it bothered her.

"I suppose that does make sense." Sure I saw movement at the front window, I stepped closer to Amelia, hoping we looked intimate. "I'll get in trouble if we talk long, though."

"With Headmaster Stark or Julianna?"

"Both." I laughed.

"Then I'll get out of your hair. But, hey—have you heard anything about Bernard?"

"Bernard Arnold?" I barely knew the guy. He was a junior, fairly quiet, the broody type. "What about him?"

"He's missing."

"Missing?"

"He missed check-in, so his RA called his family, and it seems there was a mix-up—dad thought mom had him, mom thought dad had him—one of those preoccupied and divorced parent situations. They're doing some investigating with other family and friends, but basically it looks like he never left."

"So he was here the whole time." There were always a couple of students who stuck around for the shorter breaks. Scholarship kids, usually. Kids who couldn't afford a quick trip home.

"No. No one's seen him since Friday before break."

"Fuck." I glanced back at Jolie, wondering if she'd heard anything about it. "Does Stark know?"

She nodded. "I heard the dorm parent called him a few hours ago to ask if he should contact the police. Stark said to give it until tomorrow."

He was so obsessed with his image, it totally made sense. The asshole probably wanted an internal investigation so he could clean up his rep before anyone found out one of his students ran away. "Let me know if you hear anything?"

"Yep."

This was the awkward part—the goodbye. If Stark was watching, and there was a fifty-fifty chance he was since he was hyper attentive where his daughter and I were concerned—then our goodbye would be best with a little oomph.

But I hated going that far with the ruse, especially when I knew Jolie was watching.

Amelia made the decision for me, pressing up on her tiptoes to give me a quick kiss on the lips. "It's just a kiss," she said innocently when I jumped away too quickly. "Julianna can take it. Heaven knows she's not a prude."

Sensing I was already in hot water, I didn't press the conversation further. "Bye, Amelia," I said and headed back to the car.

It was obvious Jolie wasn't speaking to me before I'd tried to engage her in conversation. Hell, I couldn't get her to even look at me.

"Come on, Jol. You know it's for show." I picked up the sponge from the bucket, but I was more concerned with her than the car. "And if you're going to be mad at someone, be mad at Amelia. It wasn't me."

I felt a little shitty for throwing Amelia under the bus, but it wasn't like it wasn't the truth.

"Mm-hmm."

Yeah, definitely not speaking to me.

Which was maddening on so many levels. Did she think I liked the situation any better than she did? Did she think I wanted to be making out with Amelia instead of her?

And what about Amelia's prude comment? It wasn't the only recent reference I'd heard to Jolie's past reputation. "At least I'm front and center about it. I have no idea what you're doing with the boys you're supposedly tutoring."

That got her attention. "Are you seriously suggesting I'm messing around?"

I already felt guilty for bringing it up, but now that I had, I wasn't sure how to back out of it.

So I shrugged. "How am I supposed to know?"

"That is some bullshit, Cade Warren. I'm upset about something I saw with my own two eyes, and instead of validating my feelings about it, you decide to make up some baseless drama about me so that you can feel better about yourself?"

"Not exactly baseless..."

I deserved it when she threw the bucket of soapy water on me.

She immediately clapped her hand over her mouth, but I could see the laughter in her eyes, and because I wanted to lighten the situation—and also a little because I wanted revenge—I picked up the hose, turned on the nozzle at the end, and sprayed her.

"Oh my God, you didn't." She looked down at her soaked shirt, her back arched trying to keep the cold, wet material from her skin.

"I did." I was still wetter than she was. "And guess what? I'm about to do it again."

With a shriek, she ran backward, holding her hands up as though they could protect her.

I followed after her, getting one more good spray in before abandoning the hose and chasing her. I caught up with her easily, and no longer in the sight of the front windows, I walked her back until she was pressed up against the garage.

"It makes me so fucking crazy to have to be secret about you," I growled. Her bra was thin under the wet, white T-shirt, and I could see the details of her hard nipples clearly. "It rips me apart to not be able to tell the whole world how I feel about you."

Unable to stop myself, I leaned in and devoured her mouth. And because I really was at the end of my rope—because I was so fucking worn out from having to be restrained—I slipped my hand down her swim shorts, inside her panties, and found the warm button between her legs that I'd become so familiar with in the last few months.

"We shouldn't do this." But the tone in her voice sounded more like *please, keep doing this*, and her own hand was stroking my cock through my jeans.

"I'm so fucking tired of *shouldn't*." I slid my hand lower, probing inside of her. She was so wet, and it wasn't from the hose.

"I don't know how to stay away from you."

"Someday, there won't be anymore sneaking around. Someday, it will be you and me going on trips to the Bahamas. Someday, it isn't going to matter how we met or what we were to each other. The only label that will matter is that you're mine."

Her hand lost its rhythm, and she gave up on fondling me, instead wrapping her fingers in my shirt, clutching on as though she needed the support to stand. I penetrated deeper, adding a second finger when her walls began to tighten around the first. Concentrating on her reactions, I moved my thumb against her sensitive nub, teasing her with a mixture of soft and hard strokes.

I was painfully hard, her breathy gasps sending more blood to my cock, and shit, it was stupid. So fucking stupid—to be kissing her so possessively, to be finger fucking her in the yard—and after the day in the locker room, I'd been so good about not being stupid with her. I only allowed myself to touch her in the middle of the night. I insisted on condoms, and if we couldn't get our hands on them, I didn't put my cock inside her, never again putting trust in pulling out. I didn't look at her at dinner. I didn't say her name. I didn't leave my room in the morning until I knew she'd already gone downstairs. I pretended I barely noticed her. I never let on that she was the only thing that ever crossed my mind.

I'd been painstakingly good for four months, and now any ounce of restraint I'd had vanished, and all I cared about was making her come all over my hand. She was there, so close, so almost there...

I don't know how I heard it. I was so completely wrapped up in our bubble—me and her, nothing else. Maybe we had an angel on our side, or maybe my ears had just become so attuned to always being on guard, whether I was aware of it or not. However it managed to register, I heard the footsteps in time, and I pulled away abruptly so that there was at least a yard between us when Stark came around the corner. "The car doesn't look done."

Jolie was used to thinking fast. She pushed away

from the garage, her breathing still rapid. "Cade chased me with the hose," she accused.

She was pretty believable as a sibling complaining about her stepbrother's antics, as long as Stark didn't look at my crotch or think too much about the flush in her cheeks or notice how swollen her lips were.

My heart racing, I took my place in the scene. "She poured the bucket on me first."

"Accidentally. God." She marched toward the car and picked up her sponge, trying to pull her father's attention. I recognized the motives of her behavior better than I used to. *See, I'm doing what you want, Dad. There's nothing to be mad at.*

But he saw something to be mad at anyway.

I didn't think he actually saw my hand down her pants or my lips on hers, because if he had, he would have made a very big production about it. But he saw *something*. Maybe it was how we were so quick to move away from each other. Or the panicked look of my posture. Or maybe he saw the same googly eyes that Amelia claimed we always had for each other.

Or maybe I was being paranoid, and he was just pissed that we weren't finished with his car. "To my office, Cade."

Jolie went pale, and even though we'd promised not to draw attention to our relationship by sticking up for each other, she did anyway. "Why him? I said I started it with the bucket."

"I heard you. Your punishment is to finish washing the car by yourself. And Cade can explain to me why he thinks it's okay to waste my water, as well as why he finds it acceptable to distract my daughter from her chores. Are there any other transgressions you want to add to that?"

I could sense Jolie wanting to say something, wanting to save me the way she knew that I would want to save her if the situation was reversed. But I gave her a quick glance that warned her to keep her mouth shut.

*Eight weeks.* I thought the words loudly in my head, hoping she'd somehow hear them. Only eight weeks, and we were gone.

Meanwhile, I'd been fucking stupid today, and even if that wasn't what I was being punished for, I definitely deserved what I got.

# EIGHTEEN

## CADE

"TAKE off your shirt and put your palms on the desk."

It didn't matter how many times I'd been in his office now, I still found my entire body tensing up as soon as I crossed the threshold.

I was even more nervous today, the adrenaline from almost being caught still running through my veins, sending my anxiety to overdrive. My tension was validated with his initial instructions—the punishment was always worse when he started with bare skin.

Spring break was definitely over.

"It will be worse for you if you try to drag this out," Stark said when I hadn't moved past the doorway.

I'd already had the fortune of experiencing what happened when I wasn't quick to respond and wasn't about to test him again. His demeanor suggested he was in one of his more sadistic moods.

Lucky me.

Taking a deep breath, I forced my feet forward, stripping off my wet shirt as I went. Instead of dropping it to the floor, I set it on the desk before placing my palms on the wood. If this was going to hurt like I thought it was, I'd want something to bite on so I didn't chew up my tongue.

And so that I didn't scream.

Not that the happenings in this room were secret to anyone else in the house, but I preferred keeping a tough image. Even if Jolie knew it was all a facade, it kept her from acknowledging how completely awful it was, and for some reason, that made it fractionally more tolerable.

Eyes facing the desk, I shook my head from side to side, knowing that the more tense I was, the worse it would feel. After one particularly bad session a few months before, I'd found a meditation book in the library that happened to include a section on managing stress. The deep breathing techniques had been useful, both when I was facing Stark's latest punishment and when I was randomly seized by inexplicable panic.

I tried one of the methods now, engaging in a three-part breath—into the collarbone, into the lungs, exhale. I only managed to get two in before I heard the drawer open—the distinct squeak telling me it was the drawer that kept the whip—and my focus was thrown. I'd been listening for the rustle of his belt, hoping that would be his weapon of choice, or even the yardstick, which he was quite fond of and didn't leave lasting damage.

The skinny-tailed whip was the worst, and my

wounds from the last time were less than three weeks old and just starting to really heal. I'd been hopeful they wouldn't scar, but if he reopened them today, there was less chance I wouldn't walk away with a souvenir. If Jolie still had Neosporin, she'd give it to me, and if not, she might know how to get her hands on more.

But I couldn't think about the later because I was still in the now, and the now required all of my attention.

*Smack!*

Stark liked to crack the whip through the air before using it on my skin. Warming up, maybe. He seemed to enjoy the shiver of fear it sent through my body as much as he enjoyed the actual torture. Anyone that suggested that anticipation was worse than the actual pain didn't know what the fuck they were talking about, but I would readily concede that it was far preferable to just get the shit over with.

This wasn't the crack of the whip, though. This was new. This was the smack of a thick cane against the desk. A cane that would surely feel a hell of a lot more substantial than the skinny-tailed whip.

It was almost impossible to suppress the instinct to run.

"You know why you're here today, Cade?" he said, slapping the cane lightly against the palm of his hand.

"Because I wasted water, sir."

In the early days, I'd argued my supposed transgressions. It was a natural defense mechanism, and even after I'd been given positive proof that it only made the punishment worse, I hadn't been able to shut my rebellious mouth.

Submitting to his power over me had never been an option until Jolie convinced me to try it. It had gone against every instinct in my body, but she'd been right. He wanted to see me on my knees—figuratively, if not literally—and the sooner I got there, the sooner he was satisfied.

*He's even quicker if you cry*, she'd said.

I still had a hard time letting him see tears. I'd discovered he also got off on bleeding, though, which I obviously had no control over.

But I could definitely lick his ass from word one. "I'm sorry, sir. It was impulsive, and I regret my actions." *Blah, blah, blah.* It wasn't even hard to sound sincere. Seconds from facing the pain, I was always genuinely regretful.

This should have been enough to get him going. Today, he surprised me.

"You think I give a shit about the water? With as much as we use to keep the grounds green, the amount you used today is negligible to our bill."

Of course, I knew that. It was a surprise that he did. Usually, *negligible* was not a word in his vocabulary. He was a tightwad, always harping on keeping the furnace no higher than sixty-eight, practically measuring out how much cereal I put in my bowl in the morning, as if he saw the world in pennies and nickels.

I hadn't realized I could get any more apprehensive, but apparently I could. My heart rate increased, and it felt like it was lodged firmly in my throat. Surprises were never good where Stark was concerned.

"Do you want to guess again?" he asked, slapping his palm again, taunting me with the way it smacked against his skin.

I really didn't want to guess again. Because if it wasn't the water, then it was Jolie. Had he seen us after all?

Well, I wasn't admitting shit. If he'd seen us, he'd have to put the accusation out there himself. I wasn't walking into a trap, and I wasn't bringing Jolie into it, no matter what he did to me.

"I'm waiting, Cade."

"It was taking too long to scrub the car," I said, knowing that wasn't it, but doing my best to paint myself as innocent of whatever it was he believed. "That was my fault too. Amelia stopped by and—"

"Since you aren't allowed to have guests when you have chores to complete, that's another infraction to add to your list, but you're still far from the reason you're here right now." He bent down next to me and clapped his hand around my shoulders, as though we were buddies. "You're a dumb one, but you aren't this dumb. You know what this is about."

"I really don't, sir." I could feel his breath on my cheek, smelled the lingering scent of the tuna fish sandwich he'd had for lunch. He wasn't usually this intrusive, and the new tactic upped my trepidation. I didn't dare turn my head, afraid my eyes would give something away. Because if he really had figured out our secret, there was no way I was leaving the room alive.

He pulled on a hair at the base of my neck, chuckling when I jerked. "You really think I'm the dumb one, don't you? Think you've been pulling the wool over my eyes for months, but let's be clear—the only reason you've gotten away with it is because I let you."

I moved from trepidation to out-and-out fear. "I don't think you're dumb at all, sir. I don't know—"

"It's okay, I know. I've seen you, Cade." His tone was suddenly gentle, coaxing. "You think I've missed the way you look at her across the dinner table? I'm a man, too. I remember what it's like to be a teen. The hormones. The way anything with tits can get you hard. And my daughter is a looker. It's understandable."

My chest hurt, and it was getting increasingly harder not to piss myself. I'd thought I'd been so careful, trying to never look at her in case I let something on. The only glimmer of hope was that he was only talking about longing looks. And so far, he was only talking about me.

I'd never been big on praying, but I started right then, praying to whatever God there might be in the sky to please not be anything more.

"I figured no harm in lustful thoughts," he continued. "It seemed to be making you miserable, but no harm in a little suffering. Good for the spirit."

That was his life mantra spoken out loud right there.

"You know what was different about today?"

I couldn't help myself—I turned my head toward him, desperate to hear the depth of the shit pile I'd gotten myself in. The word what was on the tip of my tongue, but I forced myself to continue playing dumb. "I've never looked at your daughter the way you're suggesting. Not today. Not ever."

He went on as if I hadn't spoken. "Today, you weren't just looking at her with lust. Today, you were looking at her like you thought you could have her. See the difference there? See why there's no way that can't go unpunished? Because there is no way in hell you are ever getting your filthy bastard hands on my daughter. Do you hear me?"

It was surreal how relieved I could be while simultaneously feeling the weight of his threat. But fuck, I was slack with the relief, my eyes tearing. He didn't actually know anything. He hadn't seen. He had nothing but suspicions.

But if he ever, ever knew there was more...

"You do hear me," he said, clapping my back on my previous wound so that I would jerk again. "It's so gratifying to be understood. I'll make this memorable for you, so you don't forget. Go ahead, and let it out. Tears don't look good on a man, but we both know you're just a whiny little bitch. No use pretending otherwise."

I hadn't realized I was really crying, until he pointed it out. He hadn't even struck me yet, and a puddle was forming on the desk. By the time it smacked across my back, tearing and lacerating my skin, I was sobbing.

He only hit me once with the cane, but he followed with a smack of his hand against the wound, eliciting a higher-pitched cry from my throat. I could barely distinguish the next two slaps from each other because my whole body felt like a throbbing nerve. I didn't need to have the cane across my back to be in pain. It hurt just to exist, to have the mother that I had, to have to endure these punishments, to have to hide the only joy in my life from nearly everyone around me. It hurt to understand that this had been Jolie's whole life. It hurt to know we had eight fucking more weeks to survive, and it hurt to know that, even though our future had to be better than this, it was still uncertain.

And even though we were determined to escape, it hurt to know that we would never completely break free of him—he'd marked himself on our souls. He'd broken us in places that would never be healed.

I was so consumed by my crying, I didn't realize when the slaps stopped. It was almost like coming to— the way I suddenly became alert to my surroundings, the way that only a moment before I'd existed in some plane by myself—and in the shock, I didn't think before I twisted to look for Stark. It wasn't like him to have me linger after he'd finished his abuse, but I'd never broken down before, and now that I was aware of my skin, I had a feeling my wound was pretty bad.

It certainly hurt to turn, and I winced when I did, but the pain was momentarily forgotten when I saw my stepfather. His eyes were shut, so he didn't see me. The cane was hanging from his left hand, loosely at his side, and the right was fisted around his exposed cock, jerking himself rapidly, and judging from the expression on his face, he was very close to climax.

Bile rose in my mouth, and I quickly turned back to the desk, focusing my eyes on the wood so hard they physically hurt. *Unsee it, unsee it, unsee it.* I commanded myself to forget. It was such a brief look. So brief it didn't count. Like when I picked up a cigarette that I'd dropped on the ground and told myself *five-second rule* before picking it up and putting it in my mouth.

I didn't see it.

It didn't happen.

It *couldn't* be happening.

As terrible as everything else was, this couldn't be part of it. This would make it too terrible. This would make it that much closer to unsurvivable.

At the same time, another part of my brain tried to sort the new information. Tried to be reasonable. *You always knew your pain got him going. This is probably what he does every time after you leave. This isn't anything new. This doesn't change anything.*

But it changed everything.

I knew that despite not having time or capability to process it.

I knew this had inflicted a new pain that I couldn't begin to absorb.

This thing he'd done—was doing—*to me* without even touching me, it had an immeasurable weight. This was a trauma that couldn't be scaled against the other traumas. I was desperately trying to compartmentalize it, trying to stow it someplace I'd never remember, but it was too big to tuck away neatly, so instead it occupied every part of me, and still I was already trying to block it out, trying to paint over it. Trying to make it blend in with everything else so I could pretend it wasn't there. So I could make it go away. Make it not be real.

Just look at the desk.

Just see the desk.

Don't see anything but the desk.

I stared at that one spot, and didn't move for what seemed like ages. I managed to concentrate all of my attention on my throbbing back, so I didn't hear when he finished or when he zipped up his pants or when he finally walked to the drawer to put away the cane.

"When you're done sobbing like a little girl, you can clean up your tears and get out of here," he said.

He'd been so self-absorbed, he hadn't noticed I'd stopped crying.

That was good. I was glad he'd forgotten about me. It made it easier for me to forget about him.

I pretended to wipe the last of my tears away, grabbed my T-shirt to dry up the drops on the desk, then left without putting it on. Without looking at him. I always felt small coming out of his office, along with whatever pain he'd administered that session. Today, I also felt exposed. I felt naked, like I had more than just my shirt off, and it wasn't just my back burning from the slaps but all of me that burned with red-hot shame.

*Eight weeks*, I reminded myself as I climbed up the stairs to my room. Thank God Jolie wasn't waiting for me. I couldn't see her right now, and after this, we had to be cautious as fuck.

I wouldn't go to her room tonight.

I would avoid her.

We had to stop sneaking around. We couldn't risk being caught. I'd keep my eyes down through every meal. I'd lay low and keep her safe, and I swore to myself that I would never ever say a single word about what happened in that room to anyone as long as I lived.

# NINETEEN
## CADE

I WAS ALREADY MOST of the way through my physics assignment when the classroom door opened. My seat was near the front, so I didn't notice until Ms. Coates stopped her lecture. "Yes, Ms. Stark?"

As soon as I heard her say her name, I knew it was about me.

"Could you please excuse Cade Warren? His mother is here to see him about an important matter." She was all self-confidence. Not a note of anything unusual in her voice to betray the lie.

It helped that the lie was easy to believe. Most of the students boarded on campus, so parent drop-ins were not the norm, but everyone knew who my mother was. Just because she'd never called me out of class before didn't mean it wasn't possible.

"Did the office send a note?" Ms. Coates asked,

following protocol despite the fact she was addressing the headmaster's daughter. Or perhaps *because.*

"No. His mother saw me in the hall and asked me to get him for her. Should I tell her to go to the office?"

My knee bounced under my desk, and I tried to keep my expression stone, even though I was freaking the fuck out. Whatever Jolie's scheme was here, there was every possibility it was going to blow up in her face. How could she stay so calm?

It was a needless worry because after a beat, Ms. Coates sighed. "Better take your things in case you won't be back."

It took me a second to move, a bit shocked that Jolie had managed to pull this off. Ms. Coates stared at me, waiting for me to leave before she went on, and that was all that I needed to get my ass in motion. Sticking my pencil in my pocket, I dumped my notebook and my text-book in my bag and scurried to the door where Jolie was patiently waiting, a twinkle of satisfaction gleaming in her eyes.

I followed her into the hall, neither of us speaking even after the door was closed behind us. There was no way in hell she was taking me to my mother. Carla would never dare to interfere in my school day, even if there was an emergency. I had zero doubt this was Jolie on her own, and there was something romantic about that.

But there was also an incredible risk associated, and with each step we took—each second that passed with the possibility of us getting caught—I found myself getting more and more mad.

What did I expect, though? After not talking to her for four days, did I really think she wouldn't do something like this?

Finally, she led me down the arts hall and into the empty choir room. As soon as the heavy door clicked shut, she turned to face me, and I dropped my bag to the floor, bracing myself for her inevitable rush into my arms.

A rush that never happened.

"What the fuck, Cade?"

I should have expected that I wasn't the only one who was mad. She had more right to be than me, honestly.

Even knowing that, natural instinct had me automatically jumping to offense. "Me, what the fuck? What about you? What kind of ballsy shit was that? What if Ms. Coates asks my mother why she needed me, or worse, your father? What if your father had seen us in the hall? Are you trying to get us caught?"

She rolled her eyes. "Ms. Coates never follows up on anything, and my father is preoccupied with the cops and Bernard's disappearance right now. You don't think I know how to be careful?"

Immediately, I felt guilty because of course she knew how to be careful, but also because she wouldn't have had to go to these lengths if not for me in the first place.

"And don't you dare turn this on me." She stepped close enough to poke me in the chest with her finger. "Why are you avoiding me? And don't you dare say that you aren't. You've barely looked at me since Sunday, and if you blame me for getting in trouble, fine, but at least talk to me about it instead of pushing me—"

"He knows," I said, cutting her off, knowing she'd understand immediately with only those two words.

They hung in the air, stealing the oxygen with their enormity. Admitting it made it bigger, for some reason, as if it hadn't been real enough already. The sting of the wound on my back certainly hadn't been imagined.

Her face went white. "He told you that?"

"Not in so many words."

Relief swept across her features. "He doesn't know. He *can't* know. If he knew, I would have been locked in my room permanently, and he would have definitely let me know that he knew. There is no way. There is just no way."

"He doesn't know about you," I clarified. "He only knows about me, and I've been avoiding you because I wanted to be sure and keep it that way."

It wasn't the whole truth, but it was close enough. Fear had been the main motivator. I wasn't going to admit the part where I'd also felt ashamed, and like hell was I going to tell her what had happened that had made me feel that way.

Her brows turned in, a mixture of puzzlement and concern. "What did he say to you? What did he *do* to you?" As if suddenly remembering I'd probably been physically punished, she started scanning me for injuries. "Was it your back again?"

"I'm fine. A single hit with the cane."

"Can I see?" She was already trying to turn me

around, but I grabbed her hands and held them together with mine, happy to be touching her after several days of staying away.

"I'm fine," I said again, wanting to reassure her more than I wanted to be exactly truthful. The stripe hurt all the time, a constant reminder of why we had to be careful around each other.

Her body softened, seeming to be as comforted by my touch as I was by hers. "If you're fine, then why have you been distant? I miss you."

I bent my mouth to hers, kissing her softly.

"Are you over me?"

I laughed against her lips. "Fuck, no. Never." Wrapping my arms around her waist, I pulled her tighter against me. "But we can't do this for a while. Okay? He's onto me. He's seen how I look at you."

She leaned back to stare me in the eyes. "Is that what he told you? That you look at me...how?"

"Like I want you."

"And that's all? You didn't admit it?"

"I didn't admit shit, but he—"

"He doesn't know anything. Trust me." She let out a heavy breath. "You really had me scared there for a minute."

I didn't understand why she still wasn't scared. I was. "Are you not listening to me? He's watching us. He sees something between us, at least from my side, and that means he's going to keep looking for it."

"He hasn't seen anything. He's fucking with you."

"Jolie! How are you being so cavalier about this?"

"Because he does this!" She stepped away, flapping her hands in the air in frustration. "This is how he gets in your head. He makes you think he's seen you doing something bad so that you'll turn into a paranoid wreck. Remember when he said he'd caught you looking up porn sites and wiping them from the search history?"

"I swear to God I didn't do that." I'd never even heard of the sites he'd mentioned to me, but after getting punished for the thing I didn't do, I'd been extra careful not to use the home computer for anything but schoolwork.

"Exactly! He never thought you did. He sees a thing, gets an idea, and just fucks with you."

I wanted to buy her theory. I really, really did. "But this time his idea was right."

"It doesn't matter, Cade. It only matters if you admit it. Or if you start acting stupid. Believe me, he's loving how you won't even ask me to pass the peas at dinner anymore. He's watching you squirm, knowing there's nothing between us, loving every minute of it."

"Except there *is* something between us."

She brought her hands together in a prayer shape, placed them against her lips, and let out a small hum of frustration before speaking. "He doesn't know. I promise you, he doesn't know."

I considered the likelihood that she was right. We'd been so careful, never giving anything away unless we were completely alone. And when he'd come around the house, he really couldn't have seen anything but move-ment. Most likely, he'd interpreted the water fight as two teens having fun, which was enough to piss him off. He hated anyone being happy, least of all me. So was it possible he'd taken the opportunity to make it more? Just to have an excuse to give me pain?

Considering what happened afterward, it did seem more probable that the whole thing had been about scaring me, about making me miserable so he could get off.

And I'd played right into it, walking around the house like I was afraid any step I made would set off a bomb. He had to be loving every second of it.

But if there was any chance he really thought it was true...

I ran my hands through my hair. "Okay, okay. I'm probably overreacting."

"You are, but it's cute."

"But it's not a bad idea for us to be more careful, Jol." She was back in my arms, and I turned her around so that it was her against the door and not me. So I could put my weight against her and not have to worry about the pain in my back. "We should have a plan for how we'll talk to each other if something else happens." I brushed my nose along hers. "Pulling me out of class was not the most subtle of methods."

She laughed, and I could feel her breath on my chin, the tremble of her abdomen at my pelvis making my pants tighten. "Fine. Not the wisest of moves. But I was desperate. I really missed you."

Her sultry tone made my skin feel electric. I'd gotten

so used to being in her bed every night that a few days had felt like a lifetime.

But fooling around in a classroom was not a good idea. Anyone could catch us, not just her father.

Besides, I was serious about having a plan. "We keep up the minimal interactions, but if you really need to talk to me, we should have a sign. Something our parents won't pick up on."

She thought for a moment, biting her lip as she did, making it hard for me to concentrate at the same time. "The shower curtain in your bathroom," she said. "No one goes in there but you, but I could easily have an excuse of needing to grab some toilet paper or whatever. If we need to talk to each other, we leave the shower curtain open."

Pretty clever since I always kept it closed. "That's good for you, but how will you know to go in there and look?"

"I have to walk by the bathroom on the way to my room. The door's already open. I'll make it a habit to look." Her cheeks pinked up. "I might already have a habit of looking," she admitted.

I didn't have to ask. I was equally attuned to her places. Whenever I walked in the lunchroom, I looked over to the spot she usually sat, even though we didn't have the same lunch break, just because I wanted my eyes to be somewhere that I knew she'd just been.

"So if it's open, then we meet after class at the green-house," I said. I worked there most days after school, especially now that it was spring. It was officially something I'd been assigned as a punishment, but Janice, the woman who oversaw the school gardening, had requested I stay on to help her with daily tasks, and Stark was none too happy to have me working and out of his hair. "Is it easy enough to find an excuse to come by?"

She nodded as she pressed an open-mouthed kiss on my chin. "I could come by for a fresh bouquet for the dinner table. Or even just to grab some of Janice's cookies. Really, I could stop by sometime even if the shower curtain isn't open. She'd never care."

Appealing as the idea of spending more time with Jolie was, that could not become part of her routine. "It needs to be only for emergencies."

She made a whiny sound that matched the pout on her lips.

"Jol, this is important. We have to take this seriously. There's only eight more weeks—"

"It's seven now," she corrected.

"Seven more weeks, and then we don't have to think about being careful ever again. But if your dad catches us before then?" He'd kill me. I was sure of it.

She knew it too, if her sudden seriousness was any indication. "I know. It's so close, and I want it to be here so badly. I guess I get a little stupid about it."

*God, girl. Me too.*

"The shower curtain and the greenhouse," I said, making sure our plan was solid. "And no more making eyes at me across the auditorium during assembly."

Again, she flushed, the color in her cheeks sending blood to my cock.

Her hand palming me might have also contributed. "Okay, but come to my room tonight. I've left my window open all night, every night this week, hoping you'd come, and it's not warm enough for that. Plus, I can't go this long without you."

I closed my eyes, doing my best to remember the fear that had kept me away from her for days. It wasn't hard to bring it back. The pain of it still throbbed on my skin, and thinking about it made my cock soften ever so slightly.

But there was no way I was going to make it seven weeks without her. And was there really any reason to try?

Well, we couldn't fuck in the music room. That was certain.

I placed my hand over hers, then brought it up to my lips. "I'll see what I can do about finding a condom. Now you should slip out before me. I'm going to need a minute before I can be in public."

Reluctantly, I stepped away from her. My chest ached every time I had to put space between us. Tonight, though, we'd be together. And soon we wouldn't have to be apart ever again.

# TWENTY
## JOLIE

I SAT ON MY BED, leaning against the wall next to the open window, a blanket wrapped around me to keep away the spring night chill. Where the hell was he?

I stole a peek at my alarm clock only to find it hadn't moved since the last time I'd looked. To be fair, it had only just been an hour ago that I'd been locked in. Cade always waited at least that long, just to be sure. Thankfully, my father hadn't felt a need to come in and visit with me this time, but that also meant that he'd been gone quickly, and the wait for Cade felt longer.

Mostly it felt long because it had been four days since he'd snuck in at all. I was coming off of several nights of anticipation, and my whole body was jittery, and for no reason because there was no way that my father had figured anything out about us.

Or was I just telling myself that to make myself feel safe?

I'd become so used to manipulating my own emotions, I didn't know anymore which ones were real and which ones I created.

*This isn't emotions; this is logic,* my inner voice argued. My father didn't believe that boys had crushes without being provoked. I knew from experience that if my father knew someone liked me, I'd be punished for it.

My father hadn't laid a hand on me in over two weeks. He didn't know. He *couldn't* know.

I glanced at the clock again, glad to see the number had flipped, and just then, the rap came on the glass. Bolting into action, I flung the blanket and the curtain aside, lifted the window the rest of the way, then stuck my head out and peered up to be sure Cade knew it was open.

As soon as he saw me, he carefully turned around, and I held my breath while he lowered himself down to the ledge and worked his way through the window onto my bed.

"I swear I can't breathe every time you do that," I said, throwing my arms around him. Unable to resist, I glanced down. My bedroom was on the second floor, and the back of the house had a walkout basement so it was really a three-story drop. If he fell...

I'd read once that people couldn't survive any falls over four stories, so it wouldn't kill him for sure, but that didn't mean it couldn't.

"I could climb it in my sleep." He pulled away from me and shut the window then began to pull me back to him.

I resisted. "The dresser." We'd become lazy about moving it lately. It was overly cautious, not only because we'd been doing this routine for months and not been caught, but also my father had never in my life come back to my room after he'd locked the door.

If I trusted my logic, there was really no reason to be anxious about it now.

But logic also told me that I could be wrong.

Without arguing, Cade took his place on one side of the dresser and began to tug it into place while I pushed with my shoulder. "One day he's going to come up here because he hears us sliding the dresser against the door."

"It makes me feel better." That wasn't exactly true. The only thing that made me feel better was being in his arms.

I needed to be in his arms now.

Want felt warm in my belly and between my thighs. Four months into our physical relationship, and I was still blown away by the intoxication of lust. Before him, I'd only ever thought of sex as a means of negotiation. A price paid in exchange for attention, and usually scraps at that.

With Cade, it was almost always about me first. He'd given me permission to enjoy my body, and with that permission, I'd learned I could communicate with it as well. The form of expression was still so new and unexplored that I found myself choosing it over the methods of communication I'd used all my life.

I took Cade's hand in mine and pulled him with me back to the bed, letting this action tell him what I'd kept bottled for days: *I missed you. I need you. It's me and you in this together.*

He took my lead and pressed his mouth to mine, teasing me with soft kisses. I could practically feel him debating with himself about letting it become more. Four nights without each other meant four nights without talking, and that bond between us was equally important.

But words could wait, and when he slipped his tongue inside my mouth, I sighed with relief and wrapped my arms around his neck to pull him closer. As soon as I did, he retreated—not all the way, not breaking our kiss altogether, but slowing it down. Becoming less aggressive.

It drove me insane. The push, the pull. He was so good at teasing me like that. Giving just little tastes until I was near tears with want and then feeding me a feast. It didn't take long before I was breathless and clawing at his sweatshirt, needing it off. Needing his skin on mine.

Getting the hint, he broke away to pull the dang thing off. He threw it to the floor, and before he could once again take the reins of our speed, I pulled up my nightie and climbed onto his lap, a knee on either side of his hips so I could rub the ache between my thighs against the bulge in his jeans.

I bit my lip as my clit hit just the right spot, wishing I'd thought to take my panties off before straddling him. Wondering if I could shove them to the side and still get his cock inside me.

I was pretty sure he was thinking the same sort of thing, his hands moving up to cup my breasts through my nightgown, then letting out a grunt of satisfaction as he leaned back, taking me with him.

As soon as his back hit the window frame, he jerked.

Immediately, the bubble around us burst, and I remembered our reality and the latest beating he'd endured.

"Is it still really bad? Does it need more ointment?" I'd slipped him some Neosporin before dinner, but the tube had been practically empty. "I'm pretty sure I could get an antibiotic if I faked a sore throat."

He shook his head and moved himself over so his back met the flat wall instead of the window frame, taking me with him. "Carla had something from her last toothache that she never finished. I stole those. It's healing pretty well, I think." He'd told me it was only a single stripe, but he'd still been recovering from the whipping before that.

"Turn around. Let me see it."

He shook his head, and as I stared him down, I could feel myself turning protective. He was trying to be strong, and I admired that, but if he didn't want me to see it, it meant it was worse than he was letting on, which made me even more determined to see it so that I could be sure he was being taken care of.

But what was I going to do right now? He was already taking an antibiotic, and I wouldn't be able to try to get my hands on more ointment until tomorrow. Seeing it would only stir up more anger toward my father, and he already owned too much of our time. Too much of our lives. I hated giving him even a single minute more.

Would we ever belong completely to ourselves?

With a sigh, I climbed off his lap and stretched out half on top of him, half at his side. "How long do we have to hold on?"

I knew the answer, of course. I was counting down the hours. One thousand one hundred and seventy-six to go.

But the closer it got, the less it seemed real. It didn't seem possible that my life could be any different than what it was, and I needed Cade to reassure me, to say it out loud so that I knew it wasn't just a fairy tale in my head.

"It's only two months. Less, actually. Seven weeks." He brushed his lips against my forehead. "We just have to get through seven weeks, and then we're gone."

"Tell me again how we're going to do it."

As he had so many nights before, he spoke the details of our plan, falling into an easy rhythm born of repetition. "We'll walk the stage. We'll get our diplomas. Then after the ceremony, we'll leave. We won't even go to the after-party. We'll just be gone."

"And we won't take his car."

"No. We won't take my mother's either."

We went through the rest of the routine, and I played each step in my head, envisioning us behind the wheel of Janice's old truck, worrying if it would start, imagining what we'd say if we got caught.

I felt pretty sure she wouldn't turn us in. I would be

eighteen by then, an adult. I'd known the gardener long enough to believe she'd support us there. She might even let us take the truck if we asked.

Of course, we couldn't take the risk of her saying no, but the fact that she would probably be on our side if we gave her the chance made me feel worse about stealing her truck. "We'll send her money when we can," I said, reassuring myself.

"We will. We'll be fine."

"And where will we go?"

He tipped my chin up toward him. My eyes locked on his, and I swept my tongue over my lip as I waited for his answer. He always said someplace new, and honestly, I didn't care. The truth was, we had no idea where we'd go. We had no money, no family. No jobs waiting for us. No place to stay. We were running off to be homeless and at the whim of fate, but we would be together, and I couldn't imagine anything better.

Instead of answering, he pressed his mouth to mine, his tongue tracing the path mine had taken across my bottom lip. Pulling my leg up around his hip, he turned so that his cock was once again pressing against the space between my thighs.

"I need to be inside of you," he whispered against my lips before kissing me long and deep. "That's the only place I want to go."

In sync, we began undressing, fast and furiously, a desperate eagerness growing between us. If it had been a race, I would have won, but I had less to take off, and he had the condom to retrieve from his pocket.

I sat on the bed to watch him as he rolled the latex down his cock, my pulse speeding up at the sight. For so long, I'd thought the male genitalia was ugly, and objectively it still was, but looking at Cade excited me. It was part of the gift he'd given me, that ability to find joy in sex, and the thrill went deeper than just feeling turned on. Was more profound. Seeing him naked and hard, his cock in his hand, *moved* me, and when he pushed me down to the bed, my legs wrapped around him like they belonged there.

He slipped a hand down between my legs, his fingers having learned their way around well enough that I was pretty sure he was now an expert. "Are you ready for me?"

God, yes. I'd been wet since he slid through the window.

He dragged the proof up my folds and teased the pad of his finger against my clit.

"Are *you* ready for *me*?" I arched into him, praying his answer was yes, yes, yes, because I wasn't just ready, I felt empty without him. I felt unwhole.

Hadn't that been exactly what I'd been before him? Half a person. Incomplete.

It was overly romantic to think in such platitudes. Love didn't fix all. It didn't win in the end. There was no such thing as soulmates.

But I believed it all the same.

He and I as one entity was the only sort of religion that made sense to me. I'd never seen proof of God. Prayer after prayer after prayer had gone unanswered.

But Cade Warren gave me meaning. Without him, I was simply skin and bones. With him, my soul came alive.

At no time was I more alive than when he was inside me.

And since he was taking too long to get there, as soon as I felt his tip at my entrance, I lifted my hips and invited him all the way in.

I gasped at the feel of him, my pussy clenching and clinging to his cock as though afraid he'd leave too soon, though there was pleasure in his momentary absences when he dragged himself all the way out only because he immediately pushed back in. Electricity danced down my limbs and up my spine, and as deep as he was, I wanted him deeper, needed him planted. Needed him to touch me in every way he could, inside and out, so that the memory of him would linger in my body and get me through the long hours when we had to keep our distance and watch our gaze.

Some days that memory was the only thing that got me through.

When my thighs ached the next day, it would be proof that he hadn't been a dream. When I was scared and alone and trying to think of a reason to hang on, my body would remind me that Cade Warren loved me.

I brought my palms to his cheeks and kissed him. "I love you. I love you so much."

Sometimes, I thought he got off more on the words than the rest, and with my declaration, he released, grinding into me as his orgasm took over his body.

He so rarely came before me, and he was so beautiful

doing so—his face scrunched up, his muscles tense—and I wanted to linger in that moment, wanted to savor the proof that I'd done that to him. I'd wrecked him so thoroughly with pleasure and unraveled him the same way he unraveled me, and wasn't that fantastic?

But that satisfaction was interrupted with an unexpected sound—a rattling at the door followed by a fist pounding against the wood. "What the hell is this, Julianna?"

My father.

Outside my room.

The dresser was already moving with the weight of his shoulder pushing the door.

*Shit, shit, shit, shit, shit.*

We jumped apart. I flung the window open while Cade threw on his jeans. He had his shoes in hand, but his shirt... "Where is it? *Where is it?*" His whisper felt like a yell.

"Open the door right this instant!" My father's voice boomed like he had a megaphone, and slowly the dresser was moving as he pushed harder to get in. "Goddammit, Julianna! When I get in there—"

I tuned out his threat. Whatever he dished out to me, I could handle. I'd handled him for almost eighteen years. I was a pro.

But what he'd do to Cade was a whole other story.

He had to get out of my room *now*.

He understood that as well as I did. Shirtless, he climbed up on the windowsill. "If you find it, stuff it under the bed."

I knelt on the bed, my hands laced together in front of me so that I wouldn't instinctively grab onto him and make him take me with. "Be careful." I glanced back at the door, the crack wide enough that I could see the side of my father's head as he gave another shove. "Be careful, but go!"

It was already too late.

Even if Cade hadn't hesitated to give me a reassuring nod, there wouldn't have been enough time for him to get in the position to climb out. He'd have to jump to the ground, and my heart was already in my throat, my chest splitting itself in two as I quickly reasoned which was worse: broken limbs or facing my father.

Light suddenly broke into the room as the door opened completely, and though my back was turned, I knew my father was towering behind me. The horror in Cade's expression reflected the terrifying sight. It wasn't one I had to see to understand.

"You're dead, Cade Warren." His tone turned my veins to ice, and now I had my answer—broken limbs were the better odds.

Even knowing it was the right choice, I couldn't help the scream that escaped my throat as he swung his legs out the window and fell to the ground.

I stuck my head out after him, too concerned with whether Cade was okay or not to worry about the fact that I was naked and about to be in trouble. Somehow he'd managed to land on his side. He rolled twice, then got to his feet, and while I could tell he was favoring one leg over the other, he disappeared into the dark before I could evaluate just how hurt he was.

But worry for Cade was suddenly superseded by pain as I was dragged back into the room by my hair.

"You dirty whore! You fucking whore. I knew you would spread your legs for anyone, but you had to go and prove it, didn't you?"

I didn't have time to respond before the back of his hand smacked across my face. He struck again before I'd finished staggering from the first blow.

"Trash is attracted to trash. I should have realized you'd invite him into your bed." With a roar, he used his fist this time, hitting me so hard I fell to my knees, nearly blacking out.

When I could see again, I saw him at the window, looking out at the yard. "He has no place to go. He'll show up tomorrow, and I'll take care of him then."

I wasn't sure if he was telling me or himself, but the message was clear—Cade would wait. In the meantime, he had me to deal with.

My face already felt swollen, tears were already streaming down my face. Usually, that's all he needed to be satisfied, but that was when my transgressions were small. He'd want a larger payment for this.

I was already bracing myself for it when he shut the window and prowled toward me. "Get the fuck up."

*Cade's safe,* I told myself. *Safe for tonight, anyway.*

Holding on to that thought, I found the strength to stand, trying my best to cover myself.

"You know the drill. Hands on the desk. Ass toward me."

I walked over to my desk and placed my palms down. My body tensed at the familiar sound of his belt unbuckling. It would have been worse for Cade if he were standing here. I knew that in my bones.

But it was still going to be bad for me.

# TWENTY-ONE
## CADE

I WOKE UP SUDDENLY, not sure what had woken me. I'd shivered for most of the night and only fell asleep when the sun came out. Even with the jacket I'd found hanging on the hook with the garden aprons, the temperature had been miserable. Only forty degrees, according to the thermometer hanging on the glass wall. It was definitely warmer now.

I stretched my neck from side to side. I had a kink from how I'd had to sleep, curled up inside the cabinet where the extra bags of soil were usually kept, and my ankle was throbbing so badly, I was beginning to wonder if it was broken. I tried to move it now, but it was too swollen. It needed to be wrapped. It probably needed an X-ray.

Uncomfortable as I was, I didn't think it was pain that woke me up.

I sat quietly, straining my ears.

"Cade?"

It was soft, but I heard it. Jolie's voice, quiet enough to still be called a whisper, but loud enough that I heard it in my hiding spot. It was too early for her to be done with school, and I hadn't expected her until then. Was it a trap? Cautiously, I opened the door and peeked out.

She'd passed by me, so I only saw her back, but it was definitely her. Fuck, I was so happy to see her, my eyes stung. "Jol!"

I climbed out of the cramped space and made it to a standing position just in time for her to rush into my arms.

"You're here!"

Thank God we'd chosen the spot the day before as an emergency meeting place. Even without the arrangement, I would have ended up there. I had nowhere else to go. "I hoped you'd find me. I didn't know if you'd think of it."

"I was so worried. I didn't know if..." Her voice was muffled in my jacket, but I could tell she was crying from the way her body quivered.

I wrapped my arms tighter around her. "I'm okay. Swollen ankle, but I'm okay."

At the mention of my injury, she pulled away and knelt down to examine my bare foot. I'd managed to take my shoes with me on my fall, but I didn't think I could fit into it if I wanted to.

"Shit, Cade. It's purple. Is it broken?"

"Just sprained." Maybe. Probably. "But what about you? What happened—?" Just then she stood up, and I got a good look at her face, and I didn't have to finish the question. The answer was black and blue across one side of her face.

I sucked in a breath. "Oh, fuck. Jolie."

I drew her closer, cupping her face on the side that wasn't bruised as I examined her marks. It looked like his fist had slammed across her cheekbone. She couldn't even keep her one eye open all the way.

I was going to kill him. I was going to fucking slip in the house tonight while he was asleep and slit his fucking throat with a knife.

"It looks worse than it is." She was as good at minimizing as I was. Better. "Doesn't hurt nearly as much as my ass."

Guilt sank through me like a stone in mud. I'd left her there to face Stark's wrath alone. He usually left her unmarked, but I knew what he was capable of. I knew how mad he would have been. I knew better. "I shouldn't have—"

"Stop." She put a finger up to shush me. "If you'd stayed, it would have been worse."

"Not for you."

"For both of us. I hurt when you hurt."

"Well, we're both in a fuck ton of pain right now then because I feel the same." I was suddenly very aware of the weight of it all, perched on my shoulders, and I slumped forward underneath it, resting my forehead against hers.

We stood like that, not talking, just breathing each other in and holding each other up for who knows how long. Hours, it felt like. Seconds. Time lost meaning with her. We forgot the world existed.

Right now, we didn't have the luxury of escaping like that.

I forced myself to take a step back, still holding her, just not so tight. "How did you get away? How long do you have?" I'd been hidden in the cabinet when Janice did her morning circuit through the greenhouse, and she usually didn't come out again until afternoon, so I wasn't worried so much about her.

Stark, on the other hand. I couldn't imagine that he'd have let her go to school with her face looking like it did. I also couldn't imagine that he would have let her stay home without keeping her locked up tight in her room.

"He's preoccupied," Jolie explained. "Bernard's parents got here today. He's meeting with them right now and the police. He doesn't know that I left class, and if we're lucky, he won't realize it until the school day is over."

I must have looked puzzled because she amended. "I told Ms. Stacey that my face was hurting too much. She sent me to the nurse's office, and the nurse sent me home. I ran there and got some of your stuff and then came here."

I only now noticed the duffel bag at her feet, but I was still hung up on something else. "He let you go to class with your face all bruised up? How did—?" My heartbeat felt heavy when I realized the answer halfway through the question. "He said it was me, didn't he? He made you say it was me."

The guy wasn't stupid. It was a brilliant tactic, actually. Tell the school that his wild and out-of-control stepson had attacked his daughter, then ran away, and suddenly he had everyone looking for me.

Now she was the one who felt guilty, if her tears had anything to say about it. "I didn't have a choice. He said I had to blame you or...or..."

If he'd been there right then, I would have punched *him* in the face, shown him how wild I could be.

But he wasn't there. Jolie was, and she wasn't who I was angry at.

I tugged her back into me. "You had to do what he said. You didn't have a choice."

Or maybe she did. With her face as evidence, if she and I both said something. "What would happen if you tell the truth? If you blamed him?"

Frustrated, she tried to pull away, and I didn't let her because that was the last thing I wanted. "I'm just asking the question. Wonder out loud with me, will you?"

She sighed, but she stayed. "I tried to report him once. I showed one of my teachers the belt marks I had on my back."

"What happened?"

"Teacher got fired, and I couldn't walk for a week."

I wanted to argue with her, wanted to tell her it would be different if we both went forward with the proof of our injuries, wanted to tell her that it didn't have to be like that this time, but I couldn't promise her that it wouldn't be.

It was too big a risk to take.

"You did the right thing," I said, absolving her from her guilty conscience. "You had no other choice."

I'd already decided that there was no way I could go back, but this sealed that. I would have to be a runaway like Bernard Arnold. I wondered if the police would even be called to look for me. I was already eighteen, and I had a damn good feeling that Stark didn't want me in his house again.

It was okay. It was going to be okay. We were already planning to leave. Just had to readjust our plans.

So then, what now?

Jolie leaned back abruptly, apparently following the same train of thought. "It doesn't matter, Cade. It doesn't matter what people think. We'll leave. Okay? Same plan as before, but we'll leave sooner. That's all. I should have packed some things for me, but that's fine. We have time. I can run back home now. Or...or I'll leave it all behind. I don't care about anything. Let's just go. Find the keys and go."

She was agitated and worked up, and even if she'd been calm, I would have wanted to give her what she wanted. It was definitely an option. We could go. I'd already checked to see if the keys to Janice's truck were where she'd shown me before. Like Jolie said—same plan as before. Just leave now.

But while I was unsure whether or not I'd be looked for, I was positive the cops would be sent after Jolie. She was still only seventeen. Knowing him, he'd come after her and charge me for kidnapping.

Jolie didn't need me to explain any of that. She

already knew, and no matter how emphatic her plea was to run away, I could tell she knew she was lying to herself when she fell to her knees and brought her hands up to cover her face and cry.

I dropped on my knees in front of her, once again folding her into an embrace. "It's not that long, baby." I kissed her hair and rubbed her back. "It's seven weeks. Still just as long as it was yesterday. Only difference is you're going to have to be in that house alone, and I'm sorry about that."

She started crying harder.

"Shh, shh, Jolie." I wasn't used to seeing her so broken. So much of my own strength was stolen from her, and I didn't know if I could watch her crumble without crumbling myself. "Please don't, baby."

"I can't be there without you," she said, and I realized the reality of our circumstances must be just hitting her. She'd only packed things for me, so on some level she already knew, but knowing wasn't the same as accepting. "I can't. I can't without you. I'll die."

"You aren't without me. I'm here. I'm yours. Listen to me, Jolie. Look at me." I pulled her hands down from her face, made her look me in the eye. "You know this is the only way. You know it. Tell me you know it."

She blinked at me, her sobbing paused.

"Think it through. If you don't go back, he'll find us, and then he could keep us apart forever."

She hiccupped, her chin quivering. "But what about you? You can't stay here."

"No, I can't." I didn't know where I'd go, but that was

less of a worry than what I'd survive on. I could sleep in the truck at the side of the road. I couldn't live without food for two months.

I didn't want that to be her worry. I had nothing to give her, but I could give her that.

Suddenly, her eyes widened. "The cabin! You could stay at the cabin!"

"Your father's cabin?" I'd only ever heard about it.

"Yes! You can go there!" She was excited now. "There's like a six-month supply of dry goods. You might have to break a window to get in. No, wait! He keeps a key hidden in the garage. On the boat, in a compartment by the front console. Oh, and the safe! There's probably a little bit of money in there. I think the combination is my birthday."

"Jol, I can't..." Could I? It sounded too easy.

"He won't go there again until school is out."

"How... I don't even know where it is." Or if the truck had enough gas to get to Sherman. Or how I'd figure out where Sherman was.

"The address is easy. It's Atchison Cove. Ten Atchison Cove. I was ten when he bought it, and I thought it was so cool that it was the same address as my age. Plus, it's on a big sign out in front. Ten Atchison Cove, Cade. It's only an hour away. You can stay there, and no one will know, and then come back for me."

"Come back for you," I repeated, readjusting the plan in my head. "After graduation. But I couldn't come back here." The truck would be recognizable.

"The C Town. We'll meet there. I'll find a ride."

"How?"

She shook her head like it was a trivial matter. "I don't know. Someone. There will be lots of people going that direction. Amelia! I can ask her."

"Okay. All right. I'll stay at the cabin until graduation. Then I'll come back."

"You'll come back."

"Yes."

It must not have been emphatic enough for her because she grabbed onto the jacket I was wearing, clutched on tight, as though I were the only thing keeping her from drowning. "Promise me, Cade. Promise me you'll come back for me. You have to promise me."

If I hadn't already been on my knees, her pleas would have pulled me there. "Oh, baby. I'm coming back for you. I'm coming back. I'll *always* come back for you."

I remembered the stupid pipe cleaner in my pocket, but pulling it out didn't feel ridiculous. It felt earnest and sincere. "This isn't what you deserve, Jolie." I laughed at how insufficient the comment was. "It's not even close to what you deserve, but what matters is what it means."

Taking her left hand, I wrapped the pink piping around her ring finger, once, twice, three, four times, until it was wound tightly. She was crying again, these tears falling silently and slowly down her cheeks.

"We can't have a real wedding," I said. Everyone we knew thought of us as siblings, but who did we even care about having there anyway?

"I don't care about that. All I care about is being with you."

"Be with me. Be with me always. Whether it's heaven or hell, whether we sink or swim, be with me, Jolie. Say you'll be with me."

"Yes, yes, yes." It was a litany. "Yes, yes. Yes, Cade, yes."

I stared at the pink decorating her finger. If I looked at her, I'd cry too. Shit, I might have been crying already. "One day, it will be a real ring."

"It doesn't matter. I love you." She placed her hand on my cheek, and I looked up then. "I love you," she said again. "You're everything, and I love you."

I kissed her like we had forever.

I kissed her like it was goodbye.

One of those was right for today. And then in seven weeks, it would never be that kind of kiss again.

## TWENTY-TWO
## JOLIE

DAD PULLED the car into the garage and turned off the engine, the motorized whir of the garage door closing behind us the only sound.

I didn't move.

Everything hurt. Every part of my body. It wasn't like the usual physical pain I experienced, pain caused by abuse. That kind of pain radiated everywhere as well —it could make my head throb or my stomach hurt—but there was always a center. There was always a place where the pain originated.

But my father hadn't touched me in weeks, and this pain was different.

Every part of me ached. My feet, my legs, my chest, my ribs. My face. My teeth.

My heart.

I hadn't known it was possible to hurt like this. I couldn't have believed the magnitude until I'd experi-

enced it, and for the first time in all my years, I understood what it truly meant to want to die.

My father sat next to me, seeming as unanxious to
get out of the car as I was. We hadn't spoken on the ride
back from the school, which took all of two minutes, and
we didn't speak now, letting long breaths pass in silence.

"You must be tired," he said finally, his eyes focused
somewhere vague in front of him.

Exhausted was a better word. I planned on sleeping
for a week, if he'd let me, and he might. He'd been
careful with me lately. He'd been nice—driving the short
distance so that I wouldn't have to walk in my heels, for
instance—which was almost more devastating than when
he was cruel, because they always followed each other,
and it was easier to be *in* the cruel than to be waiting
for it.

Worse, this had been a particularly long stretch for
him, going on three weeks. When the kindness dragged
out, I started to get used to it. I found myself forgetting
and making excuses and loving him. Actually loving him,
despite everything he'd ever done to me. Everything he
was still doing to me.

It was the part that made me feel the most ashamed—
that I could care so much for the person who had been
the most horrible to me.

"I am tired," I said, staring into the same nowhere
that he was staring into. He'd let me stay out late, another
example of his kindness, later than I'd ever stayed out
before.

Of course, he'd stayed at the after-graduation party as

a chaperone, so it was still a favor on his terms, but it was a favor all the same. One he would expect me to be appreciative of.

"Thank you again for letting me stay out." The words were mechanical. My thoughts were elsewhere. "What time is it anyway?"

I remembered the dashboard clock as soon as I asked and moved my eyes to check at the same time he said, "Almost one."

I swallowed hard past the ball in my throat. One in the morning. Three hours late for when I had agreed to meet Cade. Was he still sitting in that parking lot, waiting for me?

I'd thought I was all cried out, but my eyes pricked again, my vision swimming. It was too late to change my mind now. Even if he was still waiting, I'd lost any chance of sneaking away when the party had ended.

I glanced at the keys hanging from the ignition. I'd never been allowed to learn to drive. Was it something I could figure out on the fly?

I thought about Carla asleep inside the house. She'd come for the ceremony but left afterward. She'd shown little emotion over the weeks about Cade's disappearance and the accusations my father had hurled upon him, but tonight she'd been less cold. Her eyes had been sad, and when Dad had told her to perk up or take her mopey ass home after the ceremony, she'd chosen the latter.

Maybe she could drive me. I had the sudden urge to ask her. If I got her alone, if I begged, if I told her she could see Cade again, could tell him goodbye...

I closed my eyes, shutting down the inclination. I'd made my decision. I'd put careful thought into it. I'd considered every angle, every option. This was the only choice I could make. The only one I could live with.

But God, did it hurt like I would die.

With a sigh, my father opened his car door and got out. I followed his lead, letting his actions guide me since I couldn't trust my own will. Knowing he detested anything left in the car, I opened the back door and retrieved my cap and gown, wrinkled now after having been worn and discarded. Habit had me worrying that I'd be reprimanded for that, and when he was standing by me when I shut the door, I immediately got defensive.

"I should have brought the garment bag," I apologized. "I can steam it in the morning. Or tonight, if you prefer. It will be good as new."

He waved his hand dismissively, as though it was silly that I'd thought such a thing. "I just wanted to say how proud of you I am, princess. You're all grown up and graduated and making adult decisions. I couldn't have asked for a better daughter."

He put his hands on my upper arms as he bent down to kiss my forehead, and I tensed, as I always did when he touched me. My head could put moments into context, but my body didn't know when one of his nice touches would turn into a not-so-nice touch, and it often reacted before I could calm it down.

Unfortunately, he noticed. He often did, and it always pissed him off. "I can't even show you a little affection without you recoiling. I've gone out of my way for you, and this is how—"

I cut him off. "You just surprised me." I forced myself to relax. Forced myself to lean into him for a hug. "I appreciate all of it, Daddy. Thank you."

He took a beat before he returned the embrace, and I made myself go numb. Made myself focus on counting the seconds as they passed. *One one thousand. Two one thousand. Three one thousand. Four—*

Then it was over, and I could breathe again.

"Here. Let me take those for you." He took the cap and gown out of my hands, as if they were a burden to carry. Without them, I didn't feel any lighter. "Did I tell you how pretty you looked? The photographer said he got a real nice shot of you all dressed up."

He turned toward the kitchen door, then stopped when he saw the full garbage can. "Oh, shit, it's Thursday. You forgot tomorrow's trash day."

Even when he was being nice, he still was rigid. The chore had been my responsibility since Cade had left, and it didn't matter that I was tired or that I was in heels or that he was trying to win me over—if it was my job, I needed to do it.

I didn't have the energy to complain. "I better get it out then." With my elbow, I pushed the button to open the door again, then rolled the big can between the two cars, out of the garage, and down the driveway. When I got to the road, I dallied before turning back toward the house.

*If I stayed here with the trash, would the garbage truck take me too?*

I was still contemplating when a rock bounced on the road by my feet. I stared down at it, and another rock skidded by.

Abruptly, I turned around, my eyes scouring the dark landscape, looking for the source of the thrown rocks, a prayer whispering on my lips. *Please, don't be here, please, don't be here.*

But my heart was wishing for just the opposite, and I nearly collapsed with relief when his whispered shout reached me. "Jolie. Jol."

He was at the shed, crouched down in the shadows, but there was no question it was him.

Quickly glancing at the house to be sure my father was still inside, I rushed down the drive as fast as I could in the stupid dress shoes, kicking them off once I reached the grass. I was already almost to him when my brain stepped in to remind me this was over. It didn't matter. I couldn't help myself. He was here, and I had no choice but to run to him.

"Oh my God, I didn't know if you'd come out."

"You shouldn't be here," I said at the same time.

But I was in his arms, letting him hold me tight while I cried into his neck. It had been seven weeks since he'd asked me to be his bride. Seven weeks since I'd last held him in my arms. I'd imagined a million different lifetimes for him. Wrote and rewrote what happened to him next, and this was not in any of those endings.

I wasn't supposed to see him again. I'd thought I'd never hear his voice, never feel his touch.

I was practically breaking apart with relief.

I clutched him tighter, breathed him in. Had his scent changed in the last two months? It was still so...*him*...but different too. Older, somehow. More intoxicating.

Less mine.

No, no. This wasn't relief. This was torment. This was worse than never seeing him at all because his being here didn't change anything. It couldn't change anything at all.

And if my father saw him...

I tore myself away and repeated my words, as much for me as for him. "You can't be here, Cade. You can't. Why are you here?"

"I came for you. I came for you. I'm so—" He was emotional and had to swallow before going on. "When you didn't show up, I was so worried he'd found out. I thought he'd locked you up. I was ready to break into the house if I had to. Could you not get away? Could you not find a ride?"

I shook my head and tried to take a step back, but he grabbed my hands and held them between us. "What's wrong, Jolie? Whatever it is, it's okay. I'm here."

I shook my head again. "You have to go."

"We can go now. The truck's parked down the road."

"No, I can't. I can't." I pulled my hands away from him and brought them to my face as if that could stop the waterfalls of tears down my cheeks.

I felt his eyes land on my hand, the empty place where his pipe cleaner ring had sat the last time he'd left. "Jol?"

It was half a word, one syllable, and yet I could hear he was on the edge. This was my fault in every way imaginable, but I needed him to take some of the blame. I couldn't be the one who broke him. I couldn't, and yet I knew I was going to break him so hard, whether I witnessed it or not, but seeing him break...

I wasn't sure I would survive.

"Why did you come?" I asked again. "Why?" Imagining his pain had been bad enough. Seeing it was like looking in a mirror with a mirror behind me. The reflection repeated over and over. The pain went on and on and on and on.

"What are you asking? What...? I came for you, Jolie. We're leaving together. We have a plan."

Shaking my head was easier than speaking.

But it wasn't enough. He needed the words too. "That's not the plan anymore."

"Of course, it's the plan. Why are you doing this?" He stood up straighter, changing tactics. "We don't have time for this. We need to go."

"You need to go. I'm not. I'm not going."

"Don't do this, Jol. Why are you saying these things?"

I was shaking. This decision had been so much easier to get behind when I didn't have to face him. He was supposed to give up when I didn't show up. He wasn't supposed to come for me, but now that he had, I couldn't believe I'd been so stupid. So unprepared. Of course, he'd come for me, and when he was standing in front of me, I got confused. Possibilities blurred.

He saw my hesitation and took advantage. "Listen, baby. Listen." He put his hands on my hips and leaned down so we were eye to eye. "The truck is in good shape. I stole a mattress from the cabin, and the shell on the back means we can sleep in it even if it's raining, and we can be someplace warm by winter."

He meant to be reassuring, but it only brought my focus back to reality. "We have nothing to live on. How are we supposed to survive?"

"We have money!" he announced suddenly. "There was more in the safe than you thought."

Hope fluttered through me despite myself. "How much?"

"Almost fifteen hundred."

My heart sunk. "It's not enough."

"It's enough if we have each other, Jol."

God, I still believed that on some level. He'd planted that idealism somewhere deep inside me, and I longed to let it bloom.

But I didn't have room anymore to make space for that hope. Reality was a voracious weed, and it choked every other chance for growth. Love did not save the day. Love did not put food on a table. Even sleeping in the truck, how long could fifteen hundred buy us? A month? Two at most. Then what? We'd have to use our IDs to get jobs and give references, both of which would make it possible for my father to track us down.

Which he would.

He would, and none of what I had to offer was fair to Cade.

My future had been set, and I loved him too much to chain him in it with me. "You have to go. You have to go."

He stepped toward me, and I stepped back. "We belong together. I love you, Jolie. You love me."

I did love him. So much that I would let him go.

My throat hurt too much to say it. I just shook my head, over and over and over until...

"Go back to the house, Julianna." My father's voice was steady and low and menacing.

The ground dropped beneath me, quicksand pulling me down, down, down, but somehow I was still standing upright.

Cade jumped back from me automatically. Then more boldly, as though he'd recovered some strength in his weeks away from this awful house, he stepped out in front of me, shielding me. "I'm not leaving without her."

Calmly, my father looked over his shoulder at me. "I'd say that's up to Julianna."

In another life, I would have taken Cade's hand, would have stood defiantly up to the man who'd raised me, who'd tormented me and loved me and fucked me up. In another life, I would have chosen with my heart.

But this was this life.

And this choice came from my heart too.

I walked around Cade, turning back one last time. My knees felt like they were going to buckle. My back hurt all the way down my spine. My throat ached. My chest felt split in two. "You should have let me go," I whispered. "You shouldn't have come."

"Go back to the house, Julianna," my father said again, and I did. I put one foot in front of the other, over and over and over until I reached the back door. I didn't look back. I couldn't. I could only move forward.

As soon as I was inside, I sank to the floor, brought my knees up to my chest, and buried my face in my dress. If I were a stronger person, I would have forced myself to watch from the window. I deserved to see what happened. I deserved to feel whatever pain my father put Cade through.

But I wasn't that strong.

I'd already used every bit of my strength to walk away. I was already in the worst pain. It wasn't possible for me to hurt more than I already did.

So I didn't watch. I hugged myself and rocked back and forth and didn't let myself think about the time that was passing or that it had been too long or that my father might not keep his word.

The material was soaked by the time he finally pushed the door open and found me on the floor. He looked down at me with as much disgust as I deserved. "Get up. Go to bed."

He was sweating, and his right hand had blood on it, blood that wasn't his.

Grief rolled through me. Regret. Anger. "You said you wouldn't hurt him. You promised, if I stayed."

He let out a laugh—a mean, gruff, calloused laugh. "I

said I'd let him walk away. I didn't say he wouldn't be bleeding when he did."

My whole life with the man, and I still never quite learned that his terms were devil terms. The bargain made was never quite the bargain you got.

But as long as Cade walked away, I reminded myself, it was worth it.

And now he was in my past. I had to look forward.

# TWENTY-THREE
## CADE

*Present*

AFTER OUR LATE night exploring and the activities that followed in the bedroom, we ended up sleeping away the morning. The bedside clock said almost noon when I opened my eyes. I stared at it, letting my vision focus, taking advantage of the particular stillness that occurs after waking to think about organizing my emotions.

I was half on my stomach, facing away from her, but very aware of Jolie. Sharing a full bed, we were close to each other whether we wanted to be or not, but she was pressed up tight against my backside, an obvious choice. And it was...

Right.

It felt right, which didn't mean it didn't also feel complicated and temporary, because it was all of the above and more. But right was an easy place to start, and so I breathed into that, and tried to let it be.

She was awake too. The stroke of her finger up and down my back gave her away. Her touch took a deliberate pathway, and though I didn't spend much time looking at that side of my body, I had a feeling she was tracing the faint scar left from Stark's cane.

Of course, that was the mark that remained. The one I was most ashamed of. The one that I couldn't ever quite reckon with.

"What do you tell women when they ask where this is from?" Her voice was morning-hoarse and sexy, and if she hadn't been bringing up such an unsexy topic, I would have rolled over and made my way between her legs.

Too bad for the mood killer since it would be awfully nice to have a subject-changer. This wasn't a conversation I was keen to get into, now or ever. There was shit from the past that still needed closure, but this was not one of them.

I closed my eyes, even though she wasn't facing me, hoping maybe she'd think I was still asleep.

"I know you're awake."

So much for that idea.

"I try very hard not to talk to women in my bed," I said, not moving.

A beat passed. The caress of her hand didn't stop. "Then I should feel special."

It was too ridiculous to let slide. I lifted my head and looked over my shoulder, giving her my best "duh" look. Seriously? She didn't feel special? She'd shattered my heart and still somehow roped me into helping her with the most outrageous of favors. It seemed pretty fucking obvious she was pretty fucking special.

Her hand stopped moving, but she kept it against my back, warm and firm. "I wish you wouldn't look at me like that."

"Like what?" I was curious how she'd interpreted it.

"Like you don't know what to do with me."

I rolled over the rest of the way onto my back and let my head sink into the pillow with a sort of huff. Because I *didn't* know what to do with her. I didn't know what to think of her or how to feel about her, and I sure as fuck didn't know how to be with her.

"I know, I know." She propped herself up on her elbow. "I ask too much, and then I ask too much again."

Her in a nutshell. At least she was self-aware.

Staring at the ceiling, I made an attempt to be equally mindful. "I wish I wanted you to stop."

It surprised her.

It surprised *me*, but it was the truth. Maybe it was all the shit Stark put us through. Maybe he'd turned me into a masochist, because as terrible and selfish as this particular ask was, it didn't scratch the surface of what I'd do for her. I'd hate it and be miserable the whole time, but I'd fucking do it. I guessed I had no sense left when it came to her.

And now I'd just outed myself. It was my weakness,

and instead of keeping it hidden, here I was, showing it off. *Use me, Jolie. Trample me to the ground. Treat me like shit, I'm here for it. Every goddamn time.*

Honestly, she probably already knew. Still, I wanted the admission to mean something to her— wanted my loyalty to matter—but I couldn't bring myself to look at her to see her reaction. I just kept staring at the popcorn ceiling above me, breathing in. Breathing out.

The bed shifted, and in my periphery it seemed she'd taken the same pose. The silence between us was taut, a thick rope pulled so hard it was beginning to fray in the middle, and I wondered when it broke where I'd land. If I'd be standing or left in the mud.

"I'm going to ask too much right now," she said finally, and I was already feeling that cocktail of resentment and excitement that she stirred up in me. "When this stuff with my father is over, I don't want this to end with you."

The breath she let out was shaky, audible even over the sudden pounding of my heart in my ears. It was validating to know this was hard for her too, and maybe that should have been enough. Maybe it *was* enough, but fuck. Really?

*Really?*

Of everything she could ask...

"No, no, no. No." I shoved the covers off and got out of bed. I found my pants and shoved a leg inside, not bothering with underwear. "No."

"You feel pretty strongly about that."

I might feel strongly about it if it was real, but this wasn't real. "You're being nostalgic, Jol."

"I'm not."

"It's being here. In this house."

"It was before here."

I glanced at her and immediately regretted it. That downturn of her lip, that blinking of her eyelids like she might cry...

No. Wasn't doing that.

I turned my attention to finding my sweater, then putting it on, trying my best to ignore the part of my mind that wanted to play the fantasy out, see where it could lead. Consider it.

That was a stupid part of my mind. Incredibly stupid. And I intended on overruling it with the rational part of me, which was maybe only a very small part, but a very vocal part, and it knew where to draw the line. Apparently, I did still have some sense, and sense said this was too much. This was the one thing that went too far. If I trusted her that much—if I gave her whatever fragments of my heart that remained—and she fucked me over again, which she would undoubtedly do, then that was it. There'd be nothing left. I'd be destroyed.

I wasn't doing that again. I wasn't crawling away from her again.

"I know," she said solemnly. "I have no right to ask."

I spun back toward her. "You're goddamned right you don't."

"Not even a little bit."

She acted like she understood what she'd put me

through, but she couldn't possibly. She couldn't, or she wouldn't have dared ask this. She wouldn't have dared come back into my life at all.

Did she not realize how much I'd fucking loved her? "Fuck, Jol. You don't even know, do you?"

"Know what?"

I shook my head. At myself as much as at her because the stupid asshole in this scenario was me. *Me.* Me who obviously still loved her or I wouldn't care so much about her bullshit, wouldn't wonder whether it really was bullshit, wouldn't hope that...

"This isn't fucking fair, Jolie." I shoved my foot inside a boot.

"It's not."

I found the other boot and put it on. I'd been dressing so I could run, and now that I was done, I wasn't ready to leave.

I paced the length of the room. Went to the window. Turned back to her. "This is because we fucked. I told you that you'd make it more than it is."

"Am I really making it more?" She asked so earnestly, and I wanted to shut her down with a definitive yes, but the word stuck in my throat, a lie too big to get out.

I ran a hand over my beard, trying to break the lie into something smaller. "You owe me too many explanations. You have too many things you won't share." As long as she withheld pieces of herself, this was only sex. It could only be sex. "You aren't relationship material."

The last one visibly wounded her, but I refused to regret it.

And she took it. Pulling the sheet up around herself, she sat up and nodded. "You're right. I could be, though, I think. If I told you everything."

"That would be a nice fucking place to start." I'd spoken before I really thought about it, and once I gave myself a second to do so, something warm stretched across my chest. A tiny ball of hope. Would she really give me answers? Would it really change anything?

My gut said that it would probably change everything.

There was something admittedly frightening about that. Just learning my mother had helped her escape had done a number on me. I wasn't sure I could take more truth.

She bit her lip, seeming to be worried as well.

I had a feeling her worries were centered elsewhere. "You're afraid to tell me because you think I'll walk out on this. That doesn't say much in your defense."

"I don't know how it will go, honestly. I think you'll understand me better, but I can't begin to know how you'll feel, so yes. You might decide you're done with me and leave me to do this alone, and that would be fair. I know I don't deserve—"

I couldn't take any more of this line, and I cut her off. "Stop, okay? Stop with the 'I don't deserve and I'm to blame for everything' bullshit. Your father was to blame. Okay? For everything. All of it. It was his fault, and no one else's."

Now she was the one who looked hopeful. "Do you really mean that?"

Shit. Did I?

"I don't know." I'd been blaming her so long, it was hard to let that go. And yet... "I want to."

There I was again, showing her all my weak spots.

For some reason, I didn't feel that scared. Like when I'd woken up, it felt right.

I was going to need some time to process that. And to process whatever she had to tell me, but in order to do that, she had to actually tell me, and she wasn't going to do that without reassurances.

"Look." I took a step toward her, crouching down so I was on her level, close enough that I could touch her, but I didn't. "I'm in this. I'm not backing out. He needs to pay for his crimes, and if our plan backfires, I'm committed to finding another plan because it's way past time he goes down. Nothing you say to me is going to change that."

Before she could respond, my phone vibrated on the nightstand with an incoming call. I glanced over, intending to ignore whoever it was.

"Donovan," she said, apparently having looked too. "You should take it."

I didn't want to take it. I wanted to throw my cell out the window and finish this conversation. I wouldn't even bother to open it first.

"We'll talk later," she promised. "Take the call."

With a sigh that felt more like a groan, I picked up my cell. "What?"

"Hello to you too, sunshine." His voice was obnoxiously smug. "I'd expected a check-in last night and heard nothing. Forgive me for being concerned."

Fuck. I'd forgotten to let him know what was going on. I was going to need a smoke for this. "Yeah, we sort of had a change of plans." I put on my coat, made sure the cigarettes were in the pocket, then gestured to Jolie that I was headed outside. "Turns out Stark's at his cabin until tomorrow," I said to Donovan. "So Carla invited us to stay the night."

Jolie stopped me before I left with a tug on my sleeve. For a minute, I thought she was going to kiss me, but she was only handing me the keys we needed to copy. "You should probably take care of this soon too," she whispered.

"Right." Then I kissed her because it really needed to be done. "What were you saying?" I resumed the call as I left the room, shutting the door behind me.

"I said that has to be interesting," Donovan repeated, only mildly annoyed.

"That's one word for it. Turned out to be for the best since it took some time to find what we needed. Hey, hold on a second, D." When I reached the bottom of the stairs, my mother was heading toward me with an expression that said she wanted to say something. "Morning, Mom. What's up?"

"Afternoon now, actually." There was an obvious opinion about my waking time in her tone. "There's cereal in the pantry if you're interested in that. There's also eggs and deli meat in the fridge. Everything's pretty much where it's always been."

"Thanks. I think I'll hold off on food for a bit." I was about to go back to Donovan when she held up a cell phone.

"Julianna left this down here last night. She's missed a couple of calls. Should I take it up or...?"

"Maybe hold off. She's not dressed yet." It was liberating to flaunt our relationship, whatever it was, not just because it made my mother give a judgmental frown but because we'd never in our lives been able to be open.

I was smiling about it when I put the phone back to my ear. "I'm here."

"You still have space on your lower back, right? This tattoo would make a great tramp stamp."

Fucking Donovan. He'd bet that I'd be in bed with Jolie before the end of the week, and if I lost, he got to choose my next tattoo. "Yeah, yeah. Fuck you." And no way was it going somewhere people could see it. Whatever he picked was likely to be embarrassing as hell.

"Anyway." I opened the door to go outside and propped the phone between my chin and shoulder so I could pack the cigarettes.

"Oh, Cade," Carla interrupted again. "If you're going outside..." She waited until I gave her my attention. "I have groceries being delivered. Could you let the guy in when he gets here?"

"Sure." I stepped out onto the porch, letting out a sigh of relief when the door was closed behind me. It was harder to be in her presence than I wanted to admit. Thank God I had an errand to get me out of the house for a bit.

Thank God I wasn't here alone.

I lit a cigarette and spent the next few minutes bringing Donovan up to speed. By the time I'd gotten to the butt, I'd answered all his questions and promised to text him with updates, then promised to mean it this time.

I hung up just as a blue Nissan Versa pulled up in front of the house and parked. A tall kid got out of the driver's seat—well, not a kid since he was driving, but he couldn't have been older than twenty—then headed around to the trunk.

"Need some help?" I jogged down the steps, figuring I could help him bring in the groceries before I took off to get the keys made.

He seemed taken aback by the offer. "No, I got it."

Then instead of pulling grocery bags out of the trunk, he pulled out a duffel bag.

"Are you here with the groceries?" Stupid question since he most definitely was not. Visiting a student probably. Here for an overnight and came to the wrong place. It happened now and then in the past too.

He looked nervous. "No, uh. I was looking for—"

I heard the house door open behind me, then Jolie's voice, bewilderment in her tone. "Tate?"

The kid's features relaxed. "Ah. There. My mom."

# ALSO BY LAURELIN PAIGE

*Visit my website for a more detailed reading order.*

### Dating Season

Spring Fling | Summer Rebound | Fall Hard

Winter Bloom | Spring Fever | Summer Lovin

### Also written with Kayti McGee under the name Laurelin McGee

Miss Match | Love Struck | MisTaken | Holiday for Hire

---

### The Dirty Universe

Dirty Filthy Rich Boys - READ FREE

### Dirty Duet (Donovan Kincaid)

Dirty Filthy Rich Men | Dirty Filthy Rich Love

### Dirty Games Duet (Weston King)

Dirty Sexy Player| Dirty Sexy Games

### Dirty Sweet Duet (Dylan Locke)

Sweet Liar | Sweet Fate

(**Nate Sinclair**) Dirty Filthy Fix (a spinoff novella)

**Dirty Wild Trilogy (Cade Warren)**

Wild Rebel | Wild War | Wild Heart

---

*Man in Charge Duet*

Man in Charge

Man in Love

Man for Me (a spinoff novella)

---

*The Fixed Universe*

**Fixed Series (Hudson & Alayna)**

Fixed on You | Found in You | Forever with You | Hudson | Fixed Forever

**Found Duet (Gwen & JC)** Free Me | Find Me

**(Chandler & Genevieve)** Chandler (a spinoff novella)

**(Norma & Boyd)** Falling Under You (a spinoff novella)

**(Nate & Trish)** Dirty Filthy Fix (a spinoff novella)

**Slay Series (Celia & Edward)**

Rivalry | Ruin | Revenge | Rising

**(Gwen & JC)** The Open Door (a spinoff novella)

**(Camilla & Hendrix)** Slash (a spinoff novella)

### *First and Last*

First Touch | Last Kiss

### *Hollywood Standalones*

One More Time

Close

Sex Symbol

Star Struck

### *Written with Sierra Simone*

Porn Star | Hot Cop

PAIGE PRESS

*Paige Press isn't just Laurelin Paige anymore...*

Laurelin Paige has expanded her publishing company to bring readers even more hot romances.

**Sign up for our newsletter to get the latest news about our releases and receive a free book from one of our amazing authors:**

Stella Gray
CD Reiss
Jenna Scott
Raven Jayne
JD Hawkins
Poppy Dunne

# ABOUT LAURELIN PAIGE

With millions of books sold, Laurelin Paige is the NY Times, Wall Street Journal, and USA Today Bestselling Author of the Fixed Trilogy. She's a sucker for a good romance and gets giddy anytime there's kissing, much to the embarrassment of her three daughters. Her husband doesn't seem to complain, however. When she isn't reading or writing sexy stories, she's probably singing, watching shows like Killing Eve, Letterkenny, and Discovery of Witches, or dreaming of Michael Fassbender. She's also a proud member of Mensa International though she doesn't do anything with the organization except use it as material for her bio.

www.laurelinpaige.com
laurelinpaigeauthor@gmail.com

CPSIA information can be obtained
at www.ICGtesting.com
Printed in the USA
LVHW032306210821
695820LV00008B/551

9 781953 520685